The Cats
of Our Lives

The Cats of Our Lives

Funny and Heartwarming Reminiscences of Feline Companions

Edited by
Franklin Dohanyos

A Birch Lane Press Book
Published by Carol Publishing Group

A Birch Lane Press Book
Published by Carol Publishing Group
Birch Lane Press is a registered trademark
of Carol Communications, Inc.

Editorial, sales and distribution, rights and permissions inquiries should be addressed to Carol Publishing Group, 120 Enterprise Avenue, Secaucus, N.J. 07094.

In Canada: Canadian Manda Group, One Atlantic Avenue, Suite 105, Toronto, Ontario M6K 3E7

Carol Publishing books may be purchased in bulk at special discounts for sales promotion, fund-raising, or educational purposes. Special editions can be created to specifications. For details, contact Special Sales Department, 120 Enterprise Avenue, Secaucus, N.J. 07094.

Manufactured in the United States of America
10 9 8 7 6 5 4 3 2 1

Library of Congress Cataloging-in-Publication Data

Dohanyos, Franklin.
   The cats of our lives : heartwarming reminiscences of feline companions / edited by Franklin Dohanyos.
       p.   cm.
   "A Birch Lane Press Book"
   ISBN 1-55972-487-0 (hc.)
   1. Cats.   2. Cat owners.   I. Title.
SF445.5.D64   1998
636.8—dc21   98-35390
                                                 CIP

*This book is dedicated not to consummate cat fanciers
who serve their pets' dinner in crystal bowls, or to cat
breeders who mate cats just for the sake of money,
but to the young child who giggles while watching
her cat batting wildly at a rubber mouse dangling
on a piece of string, and to anyone who has drawn
soothing comfort from feeling and hearing the contented
purr of a feline friend while gently stroking its fur.
And, of course, to my family, who puts up with me
when I stow away for weeks at a time while
I'm immersed in chasing windmills.*

PERMISSIONS

People with insufficient personalities are fond of cats.
These people adore being ignored.

—Henry Morgan

TO: CATS OF OUR LIVES –
Best Wishes!
Garfield & JIM DAVIS

Contents

Acknowledgments

This book wouldn't be possible without the help of many people. I would like to personally thank the following: Greg Akers from Hometown TV, Dave Barry, Michigan State Senator Michael Bouchard, Judge David Breck, Jim Davis, Delta Society, Sonya Fitzpatrick, Jurgen Gothe, Karolyn Grimes, Ernie Harwell, Tippi Hedren, Colleen and Gordie Howe, Dr. Jim Humphries, Don Knotts and Francey Yarborough, Bill Ott, Ronnie Schell, Ben Stein and Alex Denman, Dr. Robert Taylor, Dawn Wells, and everyone else who gave time and support to this project.

Introduction

If I had been asked ten years ago, shortly before my thirtieth birthday, what words I thought best described cats, I would have probably answered with the following: *cunning, confusing, finicky, frustrating, lazy, limp, loathesome, mischievous, persnickety, pesky, stupid, temperamental, unintelligent, uninteresting, vengeful,* and *wimpy.* Now, before you call the publisher and angrily demand that this book be recalled, read on.

I'm truly convinced that all cats, throughout the universe, are born with the same pervading thought about life: "Whatever!" It seems that no matter how hard you try with most cats, you can't get them to show much emotion. You can call them, pet them, dangle a fuzzy catnip mouse on a string, and all you'll receive in return is a sideways glance and a tail in the air. And then, just when you've all but given up, they'll cuddle up in your lap without notice as if to keep you off balance.

If I'm going to spend any amount of time and money caring and providing for a pet, I expect to get some interaction from it. That's probably why I spent most of my life being a dog person. See, you can mess with dogs, and they don't mind. Well, most don't, at least. You can wrestle with them, ruffle their fur, hide their toys, squirt them with the hose, even grab their tongues when they try to lick you. But if you try any of these things with a cat, you're definitely asking for trouble, as evidenced by myself nearly twenty years ago.

One of the neighbors across from my parents' house had a black-and-white male tabby who was usually pretty friendly. On one particular summer morning my neighbor and I were sitting in his backyard discussing baseball. His cat walked over and sat down next to my chair. I reached down and began scratching his ear, patting his head, and generally playing around. The cat was purring and everything seemed fine. When I got up to leave, however, the cat began clawing his way up my right arm, leaving long gashes and a steady trickle of blood. The cuts required medical treatment from the local hospital.

Now, that wouldn't have happened with a dog. Dogs get over the crazy things you do to them. They take it all in stride. It's playtime! But not cats. Cats not only don't forget the things you do, they find ways to get even. Some of these ways are immediately obvious, like tearing up the drapes, clawing the furniture, or destroying your favorite houseplant. Others, however, take a while to reveal themselves, like when you find a little kitty surprise in one of your favorite dress shoes the night of a big date, or discover that your cat has urinated in your dryer.

Despite my confrontation with my neighbor's psycho cat, I also have many happy memories with cats. A stray calico male cat appeared on my family's doorstep one day back when I was in elementary school. He was obviously hungry and tired. We kids had been told never to feed stray cats, but my sister, brother, and I couldn't resist. We fed him crackers, bread, bologna slices, and any number of odd things we could find. Eventually, we wore my parents down and they said we could keep him. That cat fit right into our everyday routines. Instinctively he knew what time school was out, and would often greet us at the corner of our street.

For those of you who took exception to my earlier use of the words *unintelligent* and *stupid* when referring to cats, you'll certainly get the last laugh at this. Shortly after my wife, Jean, and I were married, my in-laws' cat, Caterina, had kittens. We took the biggest gray male kitten and named him Blotchnik. (A joke name, obviously!) Blotchnik stayed in the sunroom all day while we were at work. I usually got home first and would let him in to the main part of the house.

One afternoon I came home as usual and opened the door to let him in. No cat. I called him, but still no cat. Great, I thought, he's gotten out. I called my wife and she said he'd been in the room when she'd left, so he had to be there. The only things in the room were a plant stand and an old upright piano, and there's no way he could've gotten into the piano. No cat is that strong! He simply wasn't in the room.

After a while, I went upstairs to change clothes and could swear I heard him mewing so I checked the sunroom again. Still no cat. I was getting pretty frustrated. I pretended to go into the house and shut the door, but remained in the sunroom. I heard a loud meow and thought I had lost my mind, because there was no cat in the room—or so I thought. It seems the previous tenant had broken a window in the room and covered it up with black plastic instead of replacing it. Blotchnik had clawed an unnoticeable slit in the bottom of the plastic, crawled through, and was contentedly sitting on the windowsill in the darkness. Score one for the felines!

Blotchnik seemed lonely by himself all day, so we decided to get him a playmate. On the way home from work one day, I saw a sign advertising free kittens. When I stopped and inquired, I was told there was one left, but it was an older kitten who had lived outdoors since birth. I figured it would be an easy adjustment for the kitten to live indoors, especially with Blotchnik. My education was about to continue! In keeping with our humorous Russian theme, we named our new cat Dosvedonya.

Soon after, we bought our first house a few miles away. We knew Blotchnik would adapt quickly, but we weren't sure how the new cat would react to being in a strange house. Before we left for work, we put her in the bathroom and closed the door. Blotchnik was in the living room. Again, I got home first and wanted to let the cat out, so I opened the bathroom door and looked around—no cat. Here we go again, I thought. I looked in the bathtub, closet, on the windowsill—I even checked the medicine cabinet. She simply wasn't there. I called my wife to see if she had been home, and she said she hadn't.

A couple of hours later I heard some faint mewing. I looked at Blotchnik, but he was sleeping. The mewing continued as I slowly walked toward the bathroom. It sounded as if it was coming from inside the pedestal sink. I began tapping on the sink—and that's when I noticed a small access opening in its base. Sure enough, that crazy cat had somehow crawled inside and gotten stuck. It took some fancy maneuvering, but I got her out. Score two for the felines!

Many non–cat lovers complain that cats don't do anything; therefore, they serve no real purpose. They just sit or sleep, taking up space. But I'm beginning to think that maybe that's the beauty of cats. You don't have to impress them with flavored pig ears or dazzle them with slobbery old tennis balls. They're content to bring pleasure and serenity to our lives by simply existing.

My father-in-law's cat is a perfect example of this. In the twelve years Jean and I have been married, I've only seen Caterina an average of twice a year. She is truly an outdoor cat and is always off chasing down something or leaving a mouse carcass on the porch as if a sacrifice in return for a bit of kibble. But to see my father-in-law and the cat enjoy each other's company when she is indoors (rare as that is) is to truly believe that cats and humans form close bonds.

Having read what I've written thus far, most people would get the impression that I don't much care for cats. *Au contraire.* Say what you will about my seeming dislike of felines, I've actually grown to like and respect them. Some of my favorite cats include Morris, Thomasina, Bustopher Jones, Sassy, Sylvester, Felix, Top Cat, Jinx the Cat, Catbert, The Cat in the Hat, Garfield, and, my all-time favorite, Tom, from the Tom & Jerry cartoons. (How many of you know and remember all these names?) Of course, I would be remiss if I didn't mention Old Deuteronomy, Rum Tum Tugger and the other characters in Andrew Lloyd Weber's spectacular musical *CATS* and Bertha's Kitty Boutique, located in Garrison Keillor's fictional town of Lake Wobegon.

So here's to the cats of our lives, those most mysterious of all household pets. They make us laugh. They make us angry. They scare us by precariously crawling along the edge of the fireplace mantel next to the heirloom Wedgwood collection one minute and calm us by gently curling up in our laps the next. Don't try to teach them tricks or predict their behavior. Just enjoy them. What they'll do next—well, your guess is as good as mine.

The Cats
of Our Lives

Some of the silliest and most humorous names I have ever heard for a cat include: Bob, Mr. Whiskers, George, Puff, Speed Bump, Chew Toy, and Mr. Wigglesworth—and the list goes on. (I'm sure you can think of a few!) The name you give your cat should, I think, describe your cat's distinct personality. Keeping that in mind, I can find no better way to start this book than with T. S. Eliot's poem, "The Naming of Cats," from *Old Possum's Book of Practical Cats.*

The Naming of Cats

T. S. Eliot

The Naming of Cats is a difficult matter,
    It isn't just one of your holiday games;
You may think at first I'm mad as a hatter
When I tell you, a cat must have THREE DIFFERENT NAMES.
First of all, there's the name that the family use daily,
    Such as Peter, Augustus, Alonzo or James,
Such as Victor or Jonathon, George or Bill Bailey—
    All of them sensible everyday names.
There are fancier names if you think they sound sweeter,
    Some for the gentlemen, some for the dames;
Such as Plato, Admetus, Electra, Demeter—
    But all of them sensible everyday names.
But I tell you, a cat needs a name that's particular,
    A name that's peculiar, and more dignified,
Else how can he keep up his tail perpendicular,
    Or spread out his whiskers, or cherish his pride?
Of names of this kind, I can give you a quorum,
    Such as Munkustrap, Quaxo, or Coricopat,
Such as Bobbalurina, or else Jellylorum—
    Names that never belong to more than one cat.
But above and beyond there's still one name left over,
    And that is the name that you never will guess;
The name that no human research can discover—
    But THE CAT HIMSELF KNOWS, and will never confess.
When you notice a cat in profound meditation,
    The reason, I tell you, is always the same:
His mind is engaged in the rapt contemplation
    Of the thought, of the thought, of the thought of his name:
      His ineffable
      Effanineffable
Deep and inscrutable singular Name.

What's in a Name?

Consider yourself a true cat fancier? See if you can match the foreign word for cat with the country it belongs to.

1.	France	a.	*Katinas*
2.	Germany	b.	*Kissa*
3.	Italy	c.	*Gato*
4.	Poland	d.	*Ga'ta*
5.	Japan	e.	*Gatz*
6.	Sweden	f.	*Pisca*
7.	Uganda	g.	*Koshka*
8.	China	h.	*Kut*
9.	Romania	i.	*Cait*
10.	Hungary	j.	*Mace*
11.	Spain	k.	*Ko-yang-i*
12.	Ukraine	l.	*Le chat*
13.	Holland	m.	*Biss*
14.	Finland	n.	*Paka*
15.	Greece	o.	*Kat*
16.	Iceland	p.	*Kot*
17.	Armenia	q.	*Cica*
18.	Lithuania	r.	*Katt*
19.	Scotland/Ireland	s.	*Kotuk*

20.	Albania	t.	*Billy*
21.	Egypt	u.	*Mao*
22.	Saudi Arabia	v.	*Neko*
23.	Korea	w.	*Gatto*
24.	Russia	x.	*Kottur*
25.	India	y.	*Katze*

Key: 1 = l; 2 = y; 3 = w; 4 = p; 5 = v; 6 = r; 7 = n; 8 = u; 9 = f; 10 = q; 11 = c; 12 = s; 13 = o; 14 = b; 15 = d; 16 = x; 17 = e; 18 = a; 19 = i; 20 = j; 21 = h; 22 = m; 23 = k; 24 = g; 25 = t.

How well did you do?

    1– 6 = one paw
  7–12 = two paws
13–18 = three paws
19–25 = four paws

In the beginning God created man, but seeing him so feeble, he gave him the cat.

—Warren Eckstein

From Cat Woman to Cat Lover

Julie Newmar

Having been cast as the feline temptress Cat Woman on the *Batman* TV series, one of my main concerns was that I knew nothing about cats—how they acted and reacted, what they were like. If I was going to *play* Cat Woman, I had to *be* Cat Woman. I had to learn what cats were all about, which was a switch, having grown up with a wire-haired terrier. As an actress, I believe that everything I do should be from a place of reality, so the more I knew about cats, the better.

My introduction to cats came when I was living in New York in the mid-1960s. June Havoc, sister of Gypsy Rose Lee, lived next to the Actors Studio and had many animals living with her whom she would rescue, protect, harbor, and care for. One day after class she invited me to see her animals, and that's where I met two of her cats. They were two of the most beautiful cats I had ever seen and I ended up adopting them. Since then I have always had two cats.

I did six episodes of *Batman* and with each appearance I felt I was becoming more catlike, thanks in large part to my two new feline friends and the three thousand or so ballet classes initiated by my mother. I've actually played a cat more than once in my life. The second time was in a pair of movies called *Oblivion* and *Oblivion II,* filmed in 1994. While Cat Woman was considered "camp," the new cat role had a more surreal style. Both movies were filmed in Romania.

Julie Newmar with one of her favorite cats

While in Romania, I requested a cat, which the director sent up to my hotel room. I was given a very small kitten. I named her Bird because she was the size of a small bird when she was given to me. Bird was an engaging cat who artfully wangled her way into a small part in the film. She was a slender, beautifully marked, black-and-white cat.

Unpretentious and less affected than most actors, she was well behaved, not nervous, and would even look at the offstage actor in individual close-ups. She was an uncanny scene stealer with her sheer poise and piercing eye contact. I was the nervous one.

I often took Bird to the set in a cardboard box with holes in it. She never tried to wriggle free or escape, not even during the long car ride. The Romanian government gave me the proper papers to bring her home to the States. My main concern was that she would have to spend twenty-two long hours in the cargo area. I thought she would never survive the cold or going without food and water. Much to my surprise she was perfectly fine—a wonderful, playful, affectionate cat, who liked to romp in all three of my gardens. Soon, though, she was prowling the neighborhood.

Alas, one day she became pregnant. I don't know which tom was the father. Some weeks later I was sleeping and, in a dream, heard a tiny squeak. I half awakened, reached up and turned on the light, and realized how fortunate it was I hadn't rolled over, for directly beneath my left ear was a wet, newborn kitten. Another was on the way, and a third soon followed. I understand that this is highly unusual, given that most cats find a hiding place, like the back of a closet, to have their kittens.

Bird had three male kittens who ate constantly and quickly outgrew her in size, so much so that they could barely fit through the cat door. After a while, in a state of fastidious self-preservation, she left my house for good. I was deeply saddened that it was me she was leaving, but I have since learned that you don't own a cat; a cat owns you.

Oddly, every year on my birthday Bird appears for an afternoon but won't come close enough for me to pet her. I still have two of her boys—Big Bird and Little Bird. But unlike their slender, discriminating mother, they are large-girthed bimbos, no doubt like their discountable American sire.

Julie Newmar is an actress who is perhaps best known for her role as Cat Woman in the TV series *Batman*. Julie recently finished a highly successful run of *Li'l Abner* on Broadway and has completed filming for a new movie, *Crossing the Line*. She lives with her two cats in Brentwood, California.

Ode to Sissy

Gail Brennan

Ode to Sissy

February 1, 1980–January 12, 1998

I remember when . . .

. . . we first saw you in the cage at the Macomb animal control office, so tiny and furry with bright eyes, six toes each on your front paws, and crying!

. . . we drove you home and in my arms you cried all the way until we put you down in the house.

. . . we wondered how to litter-box train you. You climbed into it all by yourself with no problems ever.

. . . we came home from our wedding to find dirt all over the fireplace because your dad forgot to close the basement door. I think he was a little preoccupied that day.

. . . you sat like a statue in the front window, loving to stare and keep watch, and how you would follow the sun around the house as it shone on the floor, curling up in its warmth.

. . . you were declawed. We had to pay more for those extra digits you had.

. . . any car ride or visit anywhere, especially to the veterinarian, brought such terror to you, with fur flying all over, sweaty paws, panting, and loud crying.

. . . we brought the kids home from the hospital. You were not in the least curious to see either one of them and hid when they were around; yet how excited the kids were to feed you because it was the only time you allowed them to pet and cuddle you.

. . . we got new carpeting in our first home. With all the activity going on we thought we had lost you because we couldn't find you for many hours. We went out in the neighborhood looking all over for you. Later that evening, you emerged! We never could figure out where you'd hid.

Gail Brennan and her feline friend Sissy

. . . trying to include you in our family pictures even though you hated to be picked up, having birthday cakes for you with candles, and having you sleep between our pillows, curled up and so warm. Your purr was so loud. You were family—a very special part.

. . . I wrapped Christmas presents and you thought that the ribbon and wrappings were yours to play with and drag around. You loved to sit under the Christmas tree. I hung a bell on the bottom branch so it would ring and tell us that you were there. You never caused any problems. You just loved to sit under the lights.

. . . you had surgery to remove a benign tumor on your back. You looked like a skinned rat! They shaved half the fur off your back. When I picked you up from the vet's you were so mad, and you showed it. You had the staff apprehensive and cautious. They asked that I get you out of the recovery cage instead of them. You hissed a lot, but never bit!

. . . we brought our puppy home. Her name was Maddy. We never saw you hiss so hard and loud! You would whack her with those big paws you had. You would arch your back and your fur would stand straight up. You obviously ruled the house and the dog respectfully kept her distance. She always wanted to play but all you would do is hiss. Maddy must have enjoyed it, because she would bark and wag her tail a mile a minute.

. . . every summer we would wash and blow-dry you outside. You cried through the whole bath, but at the same time you loved to be brushed. You felt and smelled so good.

. . . at the end of October 1997, your left eye began to drain and we had to take you to the veterinarian. After removal of three upper teeth and countless medications, the swelling remained. X rays were taken and we found out you had an aggressive tumor. You would eventually pass away because of it. My heart broke and I cried.

. . . you hated taking the pills and having fluids syringed into your mouth. You put up a good fight but showed your understanding by purring for me when I cuddled you. Your remaining days you slept all curled up, and would look at me when I talked to you. I kissed you and hugged you every day, and cried.

. . . I went downstairs to say good morning to you on Monday, January 12, 1998. You remained curled up and didn't move much. I gave you some water with the syringe, but you had a hard time swallowing. Because I loved you, I felt it was time. I did for you what was necessary.

. . . Dad came home at 5:30 P.M. to take you to the vet. The kids said their goodbyes and we took our last pictures together. I cradled you tightly in your yellow blanket and cried all the way. Your dad and I said our good-byes. I kissed you and thanked you for being such a good kitty.

. . . it was over. You looked like you were sleeping on the table, and for the first time, you didn't cry. I embraced you and knew that you were in a better place and at peace. We brought you home to bury you in our backyard. We wanted you with us and felt that that's what you would have wanted, too. So between our dogwood trees you were laid to rest on a frigid Tuesday evening. A cross with a medal of St. Francis marks your grave. We said a prayer for you and laid a single red rose on your grave. We both cried.

I remember now . . .

all of our good times with you throughout the past eighteen years. You will always remain a special part of my heart and I will always love you. Goodbye, old friend.

_____

Gail Brennan is a nurse; her husband, Terrance, is a doctor.
Both practice in southeastern Michigan.

No heaven will not ever heaven be, Unless my cats
are there with me.

—Anonymous

Cats, According to Dave Barry

Dave Barry

Cats are less loyal than dogs, but more independent." (This is code. It means: "Cats are smarter than dogs, but they hate people.") Many people love cats. From time to time, newspapers print stories about some elderly widow who died and left her entire estate, valued at $3.2 million, to her cat, Fluffkins. Cats read these stories, too, and are always plotting to get named as beneficiaries in their owners' wills. Did you ever wonder where your cat goes when it wanders off for several hours? It meets with other cats in estate planning seminars. I just thought you should know.

Dave Barry is a syndicated columnist for the *Miami Herald* and a celebrated author. He lives in Miami, Florida, with his family.

Cat: A pygmy lion who loves mice, hates dogs, and patronizes human beings.

—Oliver Herford

How a "Cat" Burglar Stole Our Hearts

Martin Karmel

About eleven years ago, my wife and I decided to get a cat as a companion. We looked at several but were taken by a beautiful lilac-colored Burmese kitten, whom we named Minnimore. He seemed as normal as any other Burmese kitten, I suppose. He liked to play and cuddle and would follow us around from room to room. At dinner, he would sit at the table with a napkin around his neck, prim and proper, as if he were a member of Parliament. We had no idea what lay ahead for us.

On Valentine's Day in 1990, my wife noticed something strange by our staircase. She walked over to the object and discovered it to be a pink powder puff on a stick. Neither of us had a clue where it came from or how it got there. Shortly after, there was a knock at our front door. Our neighbor, Mrs. Rowntree, had come over to reclaim her powder puff. It seems she had witnessed Minnimore escaping from her house with it in his mouth. Apparently, he had sneaked into her house through a window, grabbed the powder puff, and somehow brought it in through his cat flap.

We apologized to Mrs. Rowntree and returned her puff. As if that wasn't embarrassing enough, Minnimore went back and reclaimed his prize shortly thereafter. In fact, he has stolen it at least ten times since then.

Soon after the puff incident, we started noticing all sorts of strange

Minnimore cautiously guards some of his booty

objects appearing in our home. Minnimore was sneaking into neighbors' homes through open windows and cat flaps, and even crawling into cars to steal objects. He brought them in one at a time and gently placed them by our bedroom door or by the staircase. He would steal practically any-thing but preferred teddy bears and small furry toys, including skunks, dinosaurs, gorillas, Mickey Mouse dolls, cows, bunnies, slippers—and the list goes on. Perhaps the most bizarre item he ever brought home was a bamboo-handled feather duster over two feet long.

Once we were awakened in the middle of the night by a strange banging noise outside. We discovered Minnimore trying to push a rather large jersey sweater through his flap.

It wasn't unusual to have a neighbor come by and ask if Minnimore had brought home a certain item. Thankfully, our neighbors are good humored. Eventually we got a collection basket for Minnimore's swag and would, once a month, go door to door asking the neighbors if anything in the basket belonged to them. Minnimore tagged along with us.

We thought a companion would change Minnimore's ways. Six years ago we got Jamaica, another Burmese cat, to keep him company. Jamaica is quite different in nature from Minnimore and has apparently had no effect on Minnimore's kleptomania. In fact, Minnimore is now eleven, but still as active as ever. Winter is usually a bit of a respite for us, since Minnimore doesn't like the cold weather and everyone's windows and doors are kept shut. Minnimore has even had some public notoriety over the years. In 1996 he was awarded Cat Burglar of the Year by the *Daily Telegram.*

––––––––––

Martin and Cilla Karmel live in Tunbridge Wells, England, with their two cats, Minnimore and Jamaica. Martin is a retired banker and Cilla, a fine-art publisher. As yet, no arrests have been made!

There's no need for a piece of sculpture in a home that has a cat.

—Wesley Bates
American writer

Cat Fact Quiz 1

The Senses

TRUE OR FALSE
1. Cats can see an ant at a distance of six meters.
2. Cats can't see colors.
3. Humans hear better than cats.
4. Kittens have perfect hearing from the time of birth.
5. Kittens aren't born with a hunting instinct.

ANSWERS
1. *True.* Cats have incredible vision and in total darkness, their eyes become more like "ears," as their pupils pick up acoustic vibrations.
2. *False.* According to recent tests, cats have the ability to see color.
3. *False.* Cats are able to hear sounds that move faster than 45,000 hertz, such as the sound of bats. Humans can't hear anything higher than 20,000 hertz.
4. *False.* Newborn kittens have closed ear canals that don't begin to open for nine to ten days.
5. *True.* Hunting is not instinctive for kittens. It must be taught by their mothers.

The Human-Cat Bond: Therapeutic Cats

Delta Society

Cats have been described as aloof, independent, uncaring, wild, and even unpredictable. Yet despite these labels, the special bond between people and cats has been long believed to provide us humans with a sense of peace and comfort. Recent reports of the many benefits of human-cat interaction give credence to that belief.

First, it's a well-accepted fact that owning some type of animal satisfies our basic need to nurture, which is a real void in the lives of many people, especially those who are elderly or handicapped. Pets also require care and attention, which makes us feel needed. Second, animals are a source of fun and laughter, which is excellent therapy. Finally, animals, especially cats, are increasingly involved in therapeutic ways to help offset loneliness and depression, encourage mobility, improve self-esteem and self-confidence, reduce anxiety and blood pressure, encourage socialization, and help people who grieve the loss of a loved one.

One report details how a frail, elderly man was brought to a nursing home from a local hospital. Before the hospital, he had been discovered in a severely malnourished and confused state in a rural, unkempt farmhouse, living on Boston cream pie and other sweets. Once his condition stabilized, he was brought in restraints to the nursing home, since he refused to eat. Each day he worked to free himself from the restraints and remove his feeding tube, and each day the tube would be reinserted.

The staff was unable to break the cycle until an aide found the Home's three kittens in bed with the man. When the cats were removed, he became agitated. A reward system was devised whereby the cats would be returned to him if he ate; he then gained forty pounds and began interacting with other residents. The cats were the bridge that brought him back to reality. The director of nursing stated that without the intervention with the cats, she believes the man would have died.

In another fine example of how animals are good therapy for people, Sandra Campbell, a registered nurse with a VA facility, recently accepted a job as official "cat person" for the Somerset, New Jersey, Humane Society (now St. Hubert's Giralda) in its animal-assisted therapy program. With the cats she adopted from the shelter, she visits facilities where many of the patients are almost beyond reach, some of them with psychiatric disorders, others lost in Alzheimer's.

When a little gray kitten remained in his cage, day after day, Sandra couldn't resist. "Spunky" went home with her, a new member of the already two-cat Campbell family. Spunky's behavior was so impeccable that he passed Delta Society's skill and aptitude tests and became a "Pet Partner." Soon he was named Sandra's "pro" therapy cat, and was a regular visitor to the facilities on Sandra's list.

A year or so later, when Spunky developed severe asthma and would no longer make all his rounds, Sandra just happened to be at the shelter when Ralph, a rain-soaked, tiny orange-and-white fur ball infested with fleas but still purring loudly enough to fill the room, was dropped off. Needless to say, he became cat number four in the household and, after he passed his Pet Partner tests, and Spunky's stand-in for animal-assisted therapy visits.

As cats, their lineage is strictly alley, but as four-legged "therapists," Spunky and Ralph are legendary. With Sandra, they visit facilities such as the RAP Lounge, a nurse-administered VA unit; the Franklin Convalescent Center and Nursing Home, where many residents are Alzheimer's patients; Integrated Health Services of New Jersey; and Somerset Residence Corporation, where senior citizens and bed-bound patients alike respond positively to the cats' presence.

Sandra alternates the cat's workdays so that neither becomes "burned out." Preparation for each cat begins the night before a visit when the animal-assisted therapy carrier is put out—a clear signal that work awaits. The morning of the visit, the cat is groomed thoroughly to remove excess fur; a harness and Pet Partner tag are put on; and off the team goes.

Some of the team's greatest successes have been with patients suffering from dementia. In one case, a nonverbal patient spoke for the first time when Spunky jumped into her lap, astonishing the nurses by saying, "Pretty cat." On the next visit, with Ralph, the woman said, "What a handsome cat this is!"—proof that animals can often break through barriers immovable by humans. Spunky and Ralph are fine examples of the healing power of animals.

Hector Castaner is the proud owner of cats Buster, Flashback, and Flame, and learned firsthand about the therapeutic benefits of owning cats. He has had diabetes for over thirteen years and has found the disease very unstable and difficult to control. When his medical complications combined with a divorce, he became angry, depressed, and withdrawn. However, with his constant cat companions providing unconditional love, trust, and supportive companionship, he was able to stabilize his diabetes and began to understand the true meaning of "animals as healers." He wanted to share this feeling with others.

A psychologist for Metro Dade Human Services for fifteen years, Castaner began his Pet Partners cat group four years ago under Delta Society guidance. He began to visit shelters for abandoned children and public libraries, teaching the children to love, understand, and take responsibility for animals. His cats don't perform complicated stunts or tricks. Instead, Hector has trained them to make life easier for him by doing things not ordinarily expected from felines. "I teach cats to ride comfortably in the car, and they actually come running when they hear keys jiggling. I also train them to walk on a leash and give their paw in greeting," says Castaner.

Now frequent visitors to the Miami Children's Hospital, nursing homes, and numerous education facilities citywide, Buster, Flashback, and Flame tour the city, sharing their love with those who are most in need. "It's like therapy when they visit because I feel good all over, and I feel good the rest of the afternoon and night," says Erma Croft, an eighty-five-year-old resident of Miami's Garden Care Center. "I love it when they come because the cats get on your lap and love you, and you can tell they love you because they bring their little face next to yours and caress you."

In 1994, Castaner sent President and Mrs. Clinton a video about his work with his cats, and suggested they take the "First Cat" Socks to visit people in hospitals. In December of that year, he met Mrs. Clinton at the Summit of the Americas held in Miami. He reminded her of the video he had sent, and talked to her about animal-assisted therapy. Shortly after that meeting, Mrs. Clinton took Socks to visit the children at Washington D.C.'s Children's Hospital. Since then, Hector and the cats have received Christmas cards from the White House every year.

This story was provided by Delta Society in Renton, Washington, which has over twenty years of experience in animals helping people—people helping animals. Its Pet Partners Program trains volunteers and screens their pets for visiting-animal programs in hospitals, nursing homes, rehabilitation centers, schools, and other institutions. For more information about Pet Partners, please call 1-800-869-6898.

Four little Persians, but one only looked in my direction.
I extended a tentative finger and two soft paws clung to it.
There was a contented sound of purring,
I suspect on both our parts.

—George Freedley

The Matchmaker

Denise K. Pauley

Natalie released an exasperated sigh and stared at her computer keyboard, willing it to type a few paragraphs all by itself, like a player piano. The cursor, however, remained on a blank page, blinking impatiently. Her first attempt at writing had earned her first place in a magazine's fiction contest. Encouraged by this success, Natalie quit her secure bank job to become a full-time novelist. At times like this she began to regret her decision.

Wondering if Danielle Steele battled mental blocks, Natalie watched her six-month-old kitten, T-Bill, bat a crumpled piece of paper across the room. The gray tabby had crystalline green eyes and one white paw, which made him look like he'd stepped in a puddle of paint. He sensed Natalie studying him and pounced silently onto the desk.

"Where's your collar?" Natalie asked, scratching his stub of a chin. A month before the kitten had lost his tinkling address tag, and today the collar itself was missing. T-Bill wore an innocent look and stretched out next to the computer, harmonizing his purr with its hum. "Well, enjoy the freedom for now, because I'm ordering you a new one," Natalie said.

She abandoned the computer in search of a pet tag order form. Her search was interrupted by the whirr of a lawn mower—gardener day. T-Bill positioned himself at the front door, twitching the tip of his tail, curious to discover what the landscapers had unearthed. Natalie cracked the door open, the sunlight making them both squint. "Don't be long," Natalie said, giving his tail a shake.

From the window, Natalie watched her kitten make a decisive leap over her front gate. At dusk, T-Bill returned home. "At least one of us has a social life," Natalie said, and followed the kitten into the living room. Although her powers of creativity had vanished, her power of observation had not. Natalie noticed T-Bill was wearing a different collar—green, with a silver bell.

"Where did you get that?" she asked, wishing for the millionth time that he could speak. "This is why I make you wear a collar," she scolded. "Now someone thinks you belong to them."

T-Bill removed his new collar; he'd obviously figured out how. He brushed up against her leg apologetically, depositing wisps of fur on the hem of her jeans. He walked to the door and looked back expectantly. "Okay," Natalie sighed, "but I'm going with you. Maybe we can find out where this came from."

Her neighbor pruned rosebushes as she walked by. "Have you seen anyone with T-Bill lately?" Natalie asked.

"Nope, but I'm usually gone all day," he said. Then Natalie heard another male voice ask, "Where's your collar?"

On a porch not more than fifty feet away sat a man in his late thirties with sandy blond hair and pale green eyes. Natalie wondered why she'd never noticed him before. Then she noticed him scratching T-Bill, who was acting more like his kitten than hers.

"Excuse me," Natalie said, "that's my cat."

The man looked at T-Bill like he'd changed colors. "Your cat? He's been coming over here for weeks. I assumed he was a stray, so I've been feeding him and letting him lounge around my house."

"You've been feeding him?" She couldn't tell who looked more guilty, the man or the kitten. "He's not wearing a collar, but I guarantee you he's mine. His name is T-Bill."

"T-Bill?"

"I used to work at a bank," she said defensively.

"I've just been calling him Steel because he's gray."

"Steel?" she asked. "Funny, I aspire to be the next Danielle Steele."

He considered Natalie for the first time. She was dismayed to realize she was sporting her Los Angeles Kings jersey, no makeup, and uncombed hair. "You're a writer?" he asked.

"Trying to be." She ran a hand through her hair before extending it. "I'm Natalie."

"Chris Kendall. And you are T-Bill, I presume," he said to the kitten, shaking his white paw. With that, T-Bill trotted to Natalie, expecting to be scooped into her arms.

"Listen, I'm sorry about the mix-up, but it's good to meet you. I'm a writer, too. For the *Times*—Sports Department, actually. Are you a Kings fan?" He motioned to her jersey.

"Absolutely," she answered. "Watching hockey is my favorite diversion after sitting at the computer all day pretending to be a writer."

He smiled warmly. "Maybe we can go to the game tomorrow. I have pretty good seats . . . unless, of course, there's someone else."

"No, no one else," she returned almost too quickly. "No one but T, that is." The kitten had curled into the crook of her arm, taking them both in with a complacent gaze.

"Okay then," Chris said. "I'll pick you up around six o'clock."

Natalie said good night and practically floated home. Halfway there, she turned back to wave at Chris, then put T-Bill down so he could wander. But when Natalie opened her door, T-Bill followed, as if his days of exploring were over. Natalie smiled knowingly.

T-Bill curled up on the couch for a nap, but Natalie was too excited to sleep. Instead, she returned to the computer, its cursor eagerly waiting. This time she definitely had a story to tell—about a matchmaking kitten named T-Bill Steel.

Denise K. Pauley is a writer whose story about Natalie and T-Bill first appeared in *Cats* magazine in December 1997.

Convenience-Store Kitty

Ben Stein

In mid-1996, my wife, Alex, was driving home from her office late one evening when she decided to stop at a convenience store. Shortly before she arrived at the store, two women appeared in the street, waving their hands to get her to stop her car. They said that there was a small kitten in the middle of the street who had been hit by a car, and they were trying to contact a humane organization or do something to help her. They were redirecting traffic to protect the kitten. Alex decided to see what she might do to help.

About that same time, a man in a jeep stopped to help as well. He pulled a box from the back of his jeep and gently put the injured kitten inside. (They were all afraid to pick her up, but she needed to be taken somewhere to be humanely put to sleep.) The man closed the box and gave it to Alex. She then rushed the kitten to an emergency vet whom we know very well, because we've had five dogs. The kitten began screaming on the way so Alex put on classical music, thinking it would be a nice segue for the animal to meet her maker.

They arrived at the vet's office, and to Alex's surprise, the vet said the kitten had a very good chance of surviving, but that it was hard to tell with head injuries. The vet also informed Alex that because she had picked up a stray, the kitten would have to be released to a shelter and not to her. She would then have to make arrangements to get it from the shelter. Alex left the kitten there and drove home.

At 2 A.M. the phone rang. The vet said that the kitten would survive and that because Alex was so concerned, he was going to release the kitten to us in the morning. Up to this point, Alex had never even seen what the kitten looked like. She didn't want to see the animal in a squished state, so she'd never looked before giving the box to the vet.

So Alex and our son went to the emergency vet's office at 6 A.M. to pick up the kitten and take it to our regular vet. Besides a multitude of other problems, the kitten couldn't see or walk and had to stay at the vet's for an extended period for observation. The vet wasn't sure if the kitten would heal enough to live a normal life. We told him to do everything he could to help her.

She came home after three weeks and immediately hid under our son's bed. She wouldn't come out no matter how much we coaxed her with toys and cat treats. She stayed there for six or seven months. We put food and water under the bed for her and kept a litter box nearby. We decided to leave her alone to see what happened.

Amazingly, one day last June, Alex heard an unusual thud from another room. The cat had leaped over the Dutch door leading from our son's room and for the first time was exploring the house. It was also the first time any of us had really gotten a good look at her. She's a smallish, beautiful, tiger-striped, longhaired cat. My son named her Peabo. She's now extremely affectionate and likes to sleep on Alex's head or in bed under the covers.

Peabo gets along fine with our dogs and has seemingly picked up some doglike habits. When one of us comes home, she is always at the door, with the dogs, to greet us. She even begs for food, sometimes better than the dogs. She thinks she's one of them.

I myself was never a cat person. I've always liked dogs and couldn't believe Alex actually brought a kitten into our home. However, I was overcome by the affection Peabo showered us with. I'm happy to say we're *all* in love with her and glad she's here.

Ben Stein is an actor, author, lawyer, economist, journalist, and host of his own TV game show. Alex Denman is an entertainment lawyer with her own firm. They live with their son, Thomas, plus Peabo and a handful of dogs, in the Hollywood Hills area of California.

Tuffy, the Champion "Cathlete" of My Youth

Kim Madeleine

Cats were a big part of my life growing up in Detroit, Michigan, in the 1960s and 1970s. My family always had a cat, and each provided us with interesting experiences. My favorite of all cats was Tuffy, a twenty-two-pound Persian with paws the size of tennis balls. Tuffy was a typical cat who did regular cat things, but he was laid back about life. I suppose at his size, he didn't need to worry about much. He liked to have fun and did many humorous things. Two will always stand out in my mind.

Our next-door neighbors had a tiny Manchester dog named Coco, who had one of those high, whiny barks that drove us all crazy, especially Tuffy. One day, Tuffy was sitting on the driveway minding his own business when Coco got loose, ran across the lawn, and started yapping and nipping at the cat's feet, trying to egg him on. Tuffy was cool, though. He just sat motionless, as if nothing was happening. We believe he was allowing Coco to gain a false sense of confidence.

Coco finished his diatribe and proudly retreated to his own yard. After a few minutes went by, however, the dog came boldly running in for another attack of irksome yapping and nipping. Only this time, Tuffy was studying him. Tuffy let him get really close, and then casually and quickly whacked Coco on the side of the head with his paw as precisely as a guided missile. Coco, no match for Tuffy, rolled over twice from the impact of the paw, and sat up stunned! Tuffy casually sat licking his paw to clean it, then walked away. Needless to say, it was the last time Coco ever bothered Tuffy.

Tuffy was a playful cat and always wanted to impress us. One of the games he tried to impress us with was one we dubbed "Mouse Badminton." In this game, Tuffy would go to our backyard woodpile, capture an unsuspecting mouse, and bring it, securely clenched in his teeth, to a walkway in front of our porch.

As we sat on the porch, Tuffy would toss the mouse in the air with his mouth and whack it in full flight with one of his huge paws, just as if he had been serving a shuttlecock in a game of badminton. Or maybe even serving a volleyball.

The stunned mouse would just lie on the ground. Tuffy would casually walk over, bring the mouse back to where we were sitting, and proceed to "serve" the poor mouse again. I always tried to make him stop this seemingly cruel game, but he'd just get another mouse and start it again. Fortunately, Tuffy seemed to have a sense of fair play, and the mouse inevitably lived to see another day. I believe he really tried not to hurt them, because he realized he wouldn't have any more shuttlecocks if the mice all died. First a boxing championship, now badminton. What next?

Tuffy had a few cat friends whom he used to hang out with, especially in the summer. None was more amusing than a particular gray alley cat we nicknamed Solo, because he had lost an eye in a fight.

Solo's singular eye wasn't his most memorable trait, however. It appeared that Solo had grown up around dogs, and every time he came by our house to visit Tuffy, he'd stop by the tire of my dad's car, lift one of his rear legs, and urinate on the tire, just like a dog! I had never seen a cat do this before, and I was happy that Tuffy never picked up the habit. You can imagine the looks on people's faces when they saw a one-eyed alley cat relieving himself like a dog on my dad's car. And who says athletes don't hang around with regular people!

Kim Madeleine is a public relations and advertising professional.

Absence Makes the Bulldog's Heart Grow Fonder

Larry Stopke

There came a time, when our children were a little older, that my wife and I decided not to bring any new pets into the house. We had played guardian to more than our share of pets and wanted a break. Shortly after making that decision, the inevitable happened. A ball of fur with a rather long tail and a color scheme resembling an alley cat appeared on our doorstep. Although our no-cats-allowed-in-the-house rule had to be followed, we were nonetheless hospitable and put out food for her on the porch.

The multicolored cat was very appreciative and decided to make our porch and surrounding area her new home. Day after day we would put food out for her. Day after day the cat would travel to the children's park across the street to retrieve mouse trophies in thanks for another meal. She would often appear at the door carrying a dead mouse and deposit it on the stoop. She was a good mouser, and the relationship served both our purposes.

As summer passed and it became colder and colder, my wife refused to let the cat in the house, insisting that the cat had her own fur coat and would somehow survive. Her heart melted by December, though, when the thermometer dipped to six degrees. The cat was let in and became a respected member of the family. We appropriately named her Stranger. After a number of years we lost Stranger when she was hit by a car.

The house seemed too quiet after Stranger was killed. We decided a new pet was in order. For some unknown reason, we bought a bulldog, which we named Cecily. At about this same time, some friends we bowled with got a new kitten. As it turned out, the wife was very allergic to cats, and they decided to turn the kitten over to the local vet hospital. We, being softies when it came to kittens, couldn't resist taking the kitten into our home. We hoped that she would be as good a mouser as Stranger.

Hmmm. A bulldog and a kitten under the same roof. We didn't consider how that would work out until after we had committed ourselves to taking the kitten. We called her Caterina and hoped for the best. I soon learned how painful being an optimist can be at times! Confrontations between the two animals were a daily occurrence; neither was willing to give an inch in the territorial war, and tolerance of the other's existence was not an option. Caterina was an outdoor cat. We let her out one day and she didn't return. The bulldog had won, and was now the center of attention. While Cecily enjoyed being the queen of the household, there was a change in her. I think she had begun to miss the cat.

Early one chilly morning I awoke to meows outside my bedroom window. I figured the neighbor's cat was loose and sitting on our windowsill. I got up, put on my glasses, and looked outside. I wasn't sure, at first, but the cat looked just like Caterina. It had been quite some time since I'd seen her. I went to the door for a closer look and, sure enough, it was her. I opened the door and called her by name, and in she came. She went right to where her dish used to be on the floor.

Cecily heard the racket and came bounding into the kitchen. They looked at each other, sniffed a few times, and that was that. I swear you could see a smile cross both their faces. Never once did they fight after that. They remained friends until the end. Cecily, as sometimes happens, has since been put down due to her old age. Caterina is nearly fourteen, still with us, and one of the best mousers ever. Five years ago we got another bulldog. And so the animal education process continues at our house!

Larry Stopke is a retired electrical engineer and college instructor. He lives with his wife and two pets in Royal Oak, Michigan.

Sylvester Versus the Bag Monster

Harold Reynolds

Many stories have been told about cats that somehow manage to get themselves tangled in string, trapped in boxes, or stuck in trees. Our cat, Sylvester, managed to scare himself half to death with a plastic shopping bag.

Sylvester is a medium-size black-and-white "tuxedo" cat and rather shy. He is inquisitive, of course, and very curious. One day he was investigating a plastic shopping bag that had been dropped to the kitchen floor of our apartment in the midst of unloading groceries. For whatever reason, he stuck his head through one of the handles of the bag in order to snoop inside. When he tried to get out, however, he suddenly realized that the Awful Bag Monster had gotten him!

In a panic, he tore out of the kitchen at top speed and ran under the bed, where he is supposed to be safe from all threats, with the Bag Monster going *whop-whop-whop* on his rear. The Monster followed him under the bed, so he continued tearing around the apartment, all the while with the Bag Monster trying to eat his butt. After about fifteen seconds or so, he was able to escape its clutches when his body got through the handle. He ran for safety under the bed and didn't emerge for about an hour. He was in need of cuddles for a while after that to help him calm down.

Harold Reynolds has a Ph.D. in geography from the University of Toronto.
He currently lives with his family, and Sylvester in Toronto, Canada.

The Reeses Cat

Jill Maloney

My fiancé, Tony, and I moved from New York to Seattle, Washington, a few months after graduating from college. We were both starting new jobs as engineers for the Boeing Company. Neither of us had ever had a cat before, but I had always wanted one. About two months after the move we were driving home from a day in the mountains when Tony told me that he wanted a cat, too. I was thrilled! Of course, I had to have one immediately. When we got home we checked the papers and every other source we could find. Unfortunately, we just couldn't find any kittens. But at last we found someone who had six young kittens—one black and five orange. We decided that we would take the black one, and drove up to get him.

When we arrived and saw all those adorable orange kittens, we both decided we had to have an orange one instead—but *which* orange one? Four were rolling and playing on the floor, like fuzzy oranges bouncing around, but one orange kitten sat at our feet looking up at us. His eyes followed us everywhere, and we just had to have him. In a way, I think that it was *he* who chose *us*.

We had a hard time deciding on a name for our little kitten. We thought about Pumpkin or Peanut, but just couldn't make up our minds. One day, Tony thought of the name Reeses. It was perfect. After all, we both love the candy, and it just seemed to fit our kitten. So Reeses it was—short for Reese's Pieces.

Reeses is just over one year old now, and very playful. He loves to be around people, and loves to cuddle. He sleeps on my pillow at night, and likes to wake us up by cleaning our faces. (We don't appreciate this on the weekends!) Reeses also "helps" us get ready for work in the morning. He used to steal our socks but luckily has given up this habit. Of course, we buy him all sorts of fancy toys, but they only hold his interest for a few days. Instead, he finds his own treasures—cotton balls, Q-tips, the plastic rings from the caps of milk gallons, and toilet paper tubes.

Strangely, one of his favorite things is dental floss. No matter where he is, asleep or awake, he can tell when someone is using it. When the bathroom drawer opens, he stops what he is doing and listens. If he hears the floss being pulled out of its box, he flies across the house into the bathroom and purrs like mad. Reeses sits and happily watches us floss our teeth. He tries to help by twanging the floss or by batting at dangling ends. Then he likes to play dentist, and checks for cavities—he sticks his head in our mouths so he can see where the floss is! It is funny to watch, but really slows down the process.

Tony and I flew home to New York for Christmas in 1997. Of course, we wanted Reeses to meet everyone, so he came along. He had a little soft-sided carrier that fit right under the seat in front of us. We didn't let him sleep much the day before, hoping that he'd sleep most of the flight home. Silly us. This was his big adventure! He was very wide eyed at the airport because there was so much going on. He seemed to take it all in stride, though, and let out soft meows occasionally to let us know he was okay.

Once in the air, we put his carrier on our laps so that he would be able to see us and be more relaxed. He still didn't want to sleep, and watched the flight attendants walk up and down the aisles. When we were about to land we put him back under the seat in front of us. He didn't like this, because he couldn't see what was going on. A few minutes later, I felt something on my leg and soft fur with my hand. I looked down, and Reeses was sitting on our laps! Somehow he had managed to open the zipper on his carrier. It was very funny, and the people around us were quite amused. The poor guy had to go back in, but we were glad to be able to hug him, if only for a minute.

Now that we have a cat, it is hard to imagine life without one. We love Reeses so much! He runs to the door when we get home and purrs when we pick him up. He knows when we don't feel well and comes along with a kiss and sleeps next to us. He seems to know if we've had a bad day and wants to cuddle to cheer us up. He sleeps in the bathroom sink and loves to drink from the faucets. Reeses shreds the newspaper and likes to sit on warm pizza boxes. We love his silly little habits and his soft furry kisses. He has made our lives so much more complete!

Jill Maloney and her fiancé, Tony, live in the Seattle, Washington, area and work as engineers for the Boeing Corporation. Reeses has never gotten over his obsession with dental floss and clean teeth!

Reeses the Cat with one of his favorite treats

Socks: The "First Cat"

I don't think I could have assembled a book on cats without including a picture of the presidential cat, Socks. This picture of the First Cat was taken on the White House lawn.

Socks, the first cat

Felix the Cat:
Never Out of Style

Before Jim Davis drew Garfield and Tex Avery created Tom & Jerry, and long before Walt Disney dreamed of a talking mouse, there was Felix the Cat. Created by Otto Messmer and Pat Sullivan in 1919, Felix was based on then-popular comic actors Charlie Chaplin and Buster Keaton. Short animated films such as *Feline Follies, All Puzzled, Dines and Pines, Flim Flam Films,* and *Sure Locked Holes* established Felix as one of the greats.

A young, talented artist named Joe Oriolo joined the Felix staff in 1924 and by 1926, Felix was known by virtually everyone. He was being heavily advertised and merchandised, and songs were being written about him. In the mid-1930s, he had his own comic strip.

It's a little-known fact to most people, but Felix was television's first star. In 1940, a papier mâché likeness of him was used to test a broadcast from New York to Kansas. The broadcast originated from the world's first TV station, WZXBS, in New York. But Felix's real TV career began in 1958 with the *Felix the Cat* show, which was produced and directed by Joe Oriolo. The show included new characters like The Professor, Rock Bottom, Poindexter, and The Master Cylander.

Today, under the direction of Don Oriolo, Felix is enjoying another wave of popularity as a new generation discovers his latest cartoons and an older generation rediscovers him.

Variations of Felix

Very Old Felix

Classic Felix

New Felix

Cat and Mouse in Partnership

The Brothers Grimm

A cat, having met with a mouse, professed such a great love and friendship for her that the mouse at last agreed that they should keep house together.

"We must store provisions for the winter," said the cat, "or we will go hungry, and you, little mouse, must not stir out, or you will be caught in a trap."

They decided to buy a large pot of honey. At first, they could not tell where to put it for safety. After long consideration the cat said there could not be a better place than the church, for nobody would steal from there, so they put the pot under the altar and agreed not to touch it until they were really in want. But before long the cat was seized with a great desire to taste it.

"Listen to me, little mouse," said he, "I have been asked by my cousin to stand godfather to a little son she has brought into the world. He is white with brown spots. They want to have the christening today, so let me go to it, and you stay at home and keep house."

"Oh yes, certainly," answered the mouse, "pray go by all means. And when you are feasting on good food and things, think of me. I should so like a drop of sweet red wine."

But there was not a word of truth in all this. The cat had no cousin nor had he been asked to stand godfather. He went to the church, straight up to the little pot under the altar, and licked the honey off the top. Then he took a walk over to the roofs of the town, saw his acquaintances, stretched himself in the sun, and licked his whiskers often as he thought of the little pot of honey. When it was evening he went home.

"Here you are at last," said the mouse. "I expect you have had a merry time."

"Oh, pretty well," answered the cat.

"And what name did you give the child?" asked the mouse.

"Top-off," answered the cat, pretending not to care.

"Top-off!" cried the mouse. "What a singular and wonderful name! Is it common in your family?"

"What does it matter?" said the cat. "It's not any worse than Crumb-picker, like your godchild."

A little time after this, the cat was again seized with a desire for the honey.

"Again I must ask you," said he to the mouse, "to do me a favor and keep house alone for a day, as I have been asked a second time to stand godfather. And as the little one has a white ring around its neck, I will not refuse."

So the kind little mouse agreed. The cat crept along by the town wall until he reached the church, went straight to the little pot of honey, and devoured half of it.

"Nothing tastes so well as what one keeps to oneself," said he, smiling and feeling quite content with his day's work. When he reached home, the mouse asked what name had been given to the child.

"Half-gone," answered the cat.

"Half-gone!" cried the mouse. "I have never heard such a name in my life! I'll bet it's not to be found anywhere."

Soon after that the cat's mouth began to water again for the honey.

"Good things always come in threes," said he to the mouse. "Again I have been asked to stand godfather. This little one is completely black except his feet, which are white. Such a thing does not happen every day, so you will let me go, won't you?"

"Top-off, Half-gone," murmured the mouse. "They are such curious names, I cannot help but wonder at them!"

"That's because you are always sitting at home," said the cat, "in your little gray frock and hairy tail, never seeing the world and fancying its offerings."

So the little mouse cleaned up the house while the greedy cat went and made an end of the little pot of honey.

"Now all is finished and one's mind will be easy," he said. He came home late in the evening, quite content and comfortable. The mouse asked what name had been given to the third child.

"It won't please you any better than the others," answered the cat smiling. "He is called All-gone."

"All-gone!" cried the mouse. "What an unheard-of name! I never met with anything like it! All-gone?! Whatever can it mean?" Shaking her head, she curled herself round and went off to sleep. After that the cat was not again asked to stand godfather.

When the winter had come and there was no more food to be found out-of-doors, the mouse began to think of the honey pot.

"Come, cat," said she, "we will retrieve our pot of honey. How good it will taste, to be sure!"

"Of course it will," said the cat.

So they set out for the church. When they reached the place under the altar, they found the pot but it was completely empty.

"Oh, now I know what it all meant," cried the mouse, "now I see what sort of a partner you have been! Instead of standing godfather you have devoured it all, first Top-off, then Half-gone, then—"

"Hold your tongue!" screamed the cat. "Another word and I'll devour you, too!"

But the poor little mouse had "All-gone" right on the tip of her tongue. Out it came and the cat leaped upon her and made an end of her. Such is the way of the world.

The cat does not negotiate with the mouse.

—Robert K. Massie

Memory

Lisa Parkki

When my sister and I were growing up, we were a twosome, our parents were a twosome, and Sable, our treasured collie who liked to eat more than she liked to run, was our constant companion; the days were rich in love and laughter, in security and satisfaction, in anticipation and ambition.

I remember when our cat Stranger came to live with us. We were in high school, and the cats of our childhood had gone the way of the history books. We had had our turtle phase, our kitten phase, our dog and cat phase, our bird phase, and we were getting older and had given up childish things. Gone were the days of romping with our softball mitts, our cat by our side in the outfield; we had turned our attention to music and math, to Europe and Euripides, to boys becoming men. Cats were a closed chapter in our family chronicle.

And then she appeared one evening, mewing in the bushes near the side of the house. She was small yet composed in her state of abandonment. I did not want to see her overlooked, but there had been no unusual car passing by to explain her arrival to our neighborhood and so no clue to her origins or rightful whereabouts. Ma was firm in her resolve. "We are not having another cat," she told me emphatically.

I knew that we were too busy with our activities to take on the responsibility of raising another kitten . . . but she seemed especially appealing, an orphan who was in need but did not stoop to whining or complaining. I set out some food and drink for her, just to help her on her way, I thought to myself.

"We are not having another cat," Ma reiterated.

And so the days spilled into weeks, and the weeks poured into months, and the little cat was growing outside our house, accepting my offerings of food and drink and willing to sun herself quietly on our backyard deck. She maintained a respectful distance, apparently aware that Those in Control did not approve of her presence, but she also understood the significance of the changing of the guard in food patrol. For as the weather became colder and I got involved in the busywork of the end of the semester, Dad had begun to ensure that the cat outside still had a bite to eat and something to drink. And when the temperature at last became bitter, even Ma's heart melted to see the cat left outside when the sun went down.

So it seemed perfectly natural to name her Stranger. She came to us, but she was not one of us. She was herself. She had known deprivation, but she had also chosen companionship; and we didn't really notice when our dog Sable stopped expecting us to fling the ball back and forth to her and when she began seeking out a new furry friend. It was the beginning, as they say, of a beautiful friendship.

Then, so quickly, the endings began. My sister graduated from high school, I became an upperclassman; she went to college, I finished twelfth grade; she enlisted in the navy, and I went away to study. The days flew by like autumn leaves tumbling off the branches and skittering down the street, and we weren't home to see the "Two Old Friends" take their sunset constitutionals, sedately walking side by side as if in hobo tandem, communicating without words yet saying much between them.

Ma had witnessed it.

She had seen them chuckling together over the antics of a young pup or a cheeky bird; she had watched them tussle back and forth with a piece of cloth, just to show the whippersnappers how it was done. She had smiled to see them curled up together, nestled in each other's warmth and secure in their dreams of friendship. She had made certain that they did not eat alone. And she knew that Stranger sensed that Sable had begun to ail, that her hip joints were bothering her as often happens with collies, and that getting up each morning was becoming more and more of a painful challenge.

Sable didn't complain, and I think that was a common bond between the two. They both understood silent suffering. But then there came a time when I had returned for the summer and our dog could not get up from the kitchen floor. The moment had arrived. We had to take her to the vet, and we already knew what he would tell us.

Sable stayed in that cold, sterile place with the metal cages and the antiseptic atmosphere; she could no longer stand, and we knew the surgery would be pointless. It was time to say goodbye. None of us could bring ourselves to say it out loud.

But Stranger had not been struck dumb by this inexorable grief. She knew that her companion had been taken from the home in a state of mortal illness, and this situation was intolerable for her. She did what cats do when their world is turned inside out: She yowled and prowled and paced and panted and would not eat and would not sleep and would not rest. Her unease was eerie, her distress palpable. She knew that Sable had been separated from her with things unsaid, which needed to be spoken.

Finally, I could bear her anguish no longer. I said to Ma, "We must take her to say goodbye." Normally Ma would tell me how ridiculous my silly sentimentality was and to face reality. But this time, even Ma believed that to leave Stranger in this state would be unspeakably cruel, so she agreed to drive us to the vet's clinic.

It was a hot, sticky, humid afternoon, one of those days when you pray that your schedule takes you to a place with air-conditioning and keeps you there until the sun goes down. Our parents would never pay for the luxury of cooled atmosphere in a car because that would be a colossal waste of gas, so we had to get the cat to the clinic in a car with no air-conditioning, and with windows tightly rolled up. I was Stranger's first acquaintance in the household, so I thought that she would trust me sufficiently to lie quietly in my arms as we rode.

I had not considered the impact of long-buried memories. Because she had been abandoned by her dear friend through the use of a motor vehicle, I suspect, she had associated all manner of evil to things with four wheels. Stranger had absolutely no intention of "going quietly into that good night," and this (in her mind) was precisely the way Sable had wound up missing, so why should she stay put as long as she had four working legs? If we thought the noises she had made at home were unearthly, we were totally unprepared for her demonic conduct in the stifling-hot car—she clawed and scratched and gouged and bit and screeched and wailed and made sounds only recognizable to banshees and ghouls, and she demonstrated not one ounce of regret for imperiling my body and nearly causing Ma to drive off the road. She was fighting for her very life.

We sped us to our destination—literally. And then she knew. We were at The Place of Death. She became still, she lay motionless in my arms, and I tiptoed with trepidation to the back room with the cages where Sable was imprisoned; I didn't think I could control the cat if she got loose in the back and began to shred the surrounding pets. I should have realized that Stranger was a lady with decorum. She was fully aware of the right way to conduct a final farewell and had no intention of spoiling her friend's last moments with a maudlin display of emotion.

I walked up to the cage and let her look at the dog. Sable and Stranger exchanged a gaze as profound as it was mournful; I can attest to the fact that these two creatures, without a word, had recognized this moment for what it was and were ending their friendship in the same way in which it had begun—with love, with respect, and with true devotion to one another. In my heart I could hear Stranger tell her companion, *"Au revoir, mon amie."* That means "I will see you again. I wish you well where you are going, and I will join you there one day. Now peace, be still. You must go with God."

Lisa Parkki is a former college professor who now writes poetry,
children's stories, and fiction.

The dog may be wonderful prose, but only the cat is poetry.

—French Proverb

Grandpa's Rex Allen, the Thirty-Four-Year-Old Cowboy Cat

Jake Perry

I've always been very fond of cats and love them as much as some people love their children. I started adopting cats years ago, and since 1980 alone I've adopted well over four hundred of them. I've kept a few and found good homes for the others. Some were strays who lived around our house and others were given to me, but most of them came from the local animal shelter.

In December 1969, a German woman living in Paris, France, brought herself and her cat to visit her daughter here in Austin. When they arrived, her cat got loose and wandered off. He was picked up by a kindly gentleman and taken to the local animal shelter. Apparently the cat had been sitting by the side of the road, and the gentleman thought it might get hit.

In January 1970, I was at the shelter to adopt a few cats. I came across that stray whom the gentleman turned in and knew right away I wanted him. He was an elegant cat and looked expensive, not like the other cats there. I took him home and named him Grandpa's Rex Allen, after the old whooping, singing cowboy Rex Allen.

I wanted to find out more about him so for nearly a year I ran a "lost cat" ad in the papers. Lo and behold, a lady called one day and said she thought the cat was hers; she was able to identify him over the phone. She came by and I got to see pictures of him as a kitten and pictures of his parents. I even got paperwork identifying him as a pedigreed cat. Given

Grandpa's Rex Allen

my reputation for kindness to cats, she allowed me to keep him, but only if I agreed not to register him for showing.

As it turns out, I was right about Rex being a special cat. He was a Red Sphinx, born in Paris in 1964, and was a show cat. His registered name was Pierre. (I'd gotten used to calling him Grandpa's Rex Allen, and left it that way.)

I kept my promise and never registered him as a show cat, but he produced a fair number of offspring, who became show cats.

Years ago I bought some very good 35 mm and 16 mm movie projectors, rewind tables, and screens at an auction, added on to my garage, and converted it into a mini theater. I currently have over eight hundred films, a lot of them westerns, from days gone by. My cats love to watch the cowboy pictures because of the horses and the music. I also own a fair number of wildlife movies. Rex and the other cats often tried to chase the animals on the screen. Of course, they always met with a hard wall!

Rex fit right in with the other cats. He loved food, especially vegetables, which he had to have every day. He would eat his dry food plus broccoli, carrots, lettuce, asparagus, and more. Every morning he would get up and have bacon, egg, broccoli, and coffee. (Like father, like son.) Each year we threw a birthday party for him, complete with balloons and either a vanilla, broccoli, tuna, or asparagus cake. At Thanksgiving he and the other cats would gorge themselves so much that they ended up on their backs in the middle of the kitchen floor, snoring for hours.

Grandpa's Rex Allen died in April 1998 at thirty-four years of age. For a while, at least, he had the distinction of being the oldest living cat on record. Because of his age he was the topic of many news articles, TV shows, and magazine features. The Discovery Channel even taped a special on him. He was a natural in front of the camera and loved all the attention. He enjoyed going on rides. He knew the short ride was to the vet, which he liked, and the longer ride was to the pet supply store. It took forever to get out of the store because Rex liked to go up and down each aisle and get petted and fawned over.

I still have many cats, including some of Grandpa's Rex Allen's offspring, but none will ever replace the special bond that we shared.

———————————

Jake Perry is a retired plumber who lives in Austin, Texas, with his many feline friends and show cats.

Two things are aesthetically perfect in the world—
the clock and the cat.

—Emile-August Chartier

My Cat Leaves Me in Tatters

Don Knotts

I've spent a lifetime making people laugh through television, movies, theater, and clubs, and I've enjoyed every minute doing so. One of the basic rules of entertaining is: Don't upstage your fellow entertainers unless the script calls for it. Unfortunately, cats can't read, nor do they understand even basic English, which leads me to believe that the rules of entertaining etiquette don't apply to them—or so the cats would say!

My cat, aptly named Tatters (you'll know why later), keeps me laughing whenever I'm around her. Tatters is a beautiful five-year-old black cat with golden eyes; probably has some Siamese in her. She's an elegant cat who loves to be the center of attention, and at times she can be downright snooty. My lady friend, Francey, adopted Tatters through an Adopt-a-Pet program at a local pet supply store. Tatters is full of little eccentricities and is always making us laugh. Now and then I have to wonder who the real entertainer is around our house!

Every night before going to bed I like to have a glass of cold water. In the past, Tatters would stalk me while I was pouring and wait for just the right moment to make her move. No sooner would I set the glass of water down on the table than she would leap up, stick her face in the glass, and help herself to a long drink. After a while I wised up and started putting out two glasses of water, one for her, one for me. Still, she likes to try to fake me out to see which glass I'll go for.

Don Knotts with Tatters

As if that wasn't enough nighttime cat fun, she has another ritual, which involves trying to nibble my feet through the covers. It's a little game we have to play before either of us can go to sleep. She jumps up on the bed and waits for me to wiggle my feet from inside the covers. When I do, she bats and bites at them, as if they were a mouse.

Mornings are just as much fun. I keep Tatters's bowl full of dry food so she has plenty to eat whenever she gets hungry. Yet no matter how full the bowl is, she sits and yowls every morning until I get up and put more food in it. I'll put a few more morsels in her dish (or pretend to); then she's ready to eat. We go through these quirky, hilarious rituals every day.

Now, about the name Tatters. We have a thirty-foot ceiling with mesh curtains covering the windows. Tatters sits and stares at the curtains for a while, probably getting up her nerve, then proceeds to shoot up the curtains as if they were a tree. The problem is, she'll get really far up and then become tangled in the mesh. There she is, dangling in the air, meowing, twirling around and around, trying to escape from the curtains. There have been a few times when I thought we'd have to call 911! Hence the name Tatters—referring to the condition of the curtains, of course.

One night Tatters had us laughing so hard we had tears in our eyes. I call it "The Night of the Bag." Tatters somehow got her foot caught in the handles of a paper shopping bag, and it spooked her. She shot through the house screaming bloody murder like no one ever heard, darted under the bed, still screaming and screaming as though she was being tortured, and shot back through the house in a wild frenzy. Of course, the more she ran, the more the bag hit her in the back end, and the more panicked she became. She was dashing around, then shot back under the bed, no doubt convinced that something was trying to eat her alive! We finally caught her, removed the bag, and spent the better part of the next two hours calming her down. It was a heck of a sight!

For a while we had two cats staying with us, much to Tatters's dismay. Francey was in Los Angeles when she came upon a small kitten in a parking lot. The kitten was a mess and in obvious need of some food and a good bath. At the time, the kitten couldn't even mew. Francey took her to the vet to have her checked over, and aside from some ear mites and being malnourished, she was fine.

Now, when she first brought the kitten home, neither I nor Tatters was too happy. We had a cat and didn't need another roaming around the house. I didn't want to get close to the kitten, knowing that she wouldn't be a permanent resident here. Despite this, the kitten took a strong liking to me and followed me around like a Siamese twin. She would sit on my shoulder, wrap herself around my neck, and purr. It was like having a miniature shadow.

I have to admit, it didn't take long before I crumbled. I started to like this kitten and even began talking to her. I named her Peanut, because that's about as big as she was. I had to go on tour with a play once, and Francey told me that Peanut spent a lot of time at the door waiting for my return.

Tatters had mixed feelings toward Peanut and didn't succumb so easily to her charming demeanor. Peanut would try to snuggle with Tatters, but Tatters wouldn't have anything to do with her. One day we put them both out in the hall to play. Peanut made a dash to a stairway that Tatters had always been afraid of. Tatters took after her in an attempt to save her from the unknown terrors of the stairway—or so she probably thought.

Sadly, Peanut was found to have feline leukemia and was sent to live with Francey's mother in order to protect Tatters. We're back to being a one-cat family again, for the moment, but we do visit Peanut—who is now very healthy—as much as we can. Tatters doesn't seem too sad, though, and is back to her usual comedic, eccentric self, stealing glasses of water, climbing the curtains, and generally upstaging everyone in the house.

Don Knotts is a veteran of movies, television shows, and theater, and is perhaps best known as amiable Deputy Barney Fife from *The Andy Griffith Show.* Francey Yarborough is a stage performer. Don and Francey live in the suburbs of Los Angeles.

It is a very inconvenient habit of kittens that, whatever you say to them, they always purr.

—Lewis Carroll

St. Jerome's Cat

Anonymous

St. Jerome in his study kept a great big cat,
It's always in his pictures, with his feet upon the mat.
Did he give it milk to drink, in a little dish?
When it came to Fridays, did he give it fish?
If I lost my little cat, I'd be sad without it;
I should ask St. Jerome what to do about it;
I should ask St. Jerome, just because of that,
For he's the only saint I know who kept a kitty cat.

Mink, the Cat About Town

Denny Dawes

For years we had the most gregarious, out-and-about cat ever living in our Royal Oak glass shop. He was a long-haired gray cat named Mink. He wasn't always ours, though. Mink had a few owners here in town before he came to live with us at the store.

Royal Oak is full of neat little retail shops, restaurants, bars, and fun nightspots. There was a retail shop on the corner of the street where our building is located; the owner of that particular shop lived in Dearborn, Michigan. He found Mink behind a Dearborn restaurant eating out of the garbage and decided to take him in and bring him to work with him. This fellow had a collection of old bottles in his window and Mink, being playful and curious, accidentally knocked a few over. The owner decided to give Mink to another retail shop owner in town.

Mink was always a street-savvy cat and liked to wander around downtown Royal Oak and go visiting. He came into our store quite a bit and we loved having him around. In the winter months, when his new owner would go home for the night, we would let him stay in our store. Well, first came a litter box, then food, and then some toys. Eventually the owner came in and asked if we were feeding him, and we said yes. He said it was okay; we could even keep Mink if we wanted. He stayed with us the rest of his life. In return for our affection, Mink would bring us things. One time he brought in a small rabbit he had caught. He hadn't hurt it at all, so we returned it to the park.

Everyone had a little place in which Mink could get comfortable—the drapery shop had a special chair for lounging. Mink especially loved to go to the bar every day because it sold shrimp. He'd go early in the morning and the bartender would give him one shrimp. Mink got wise, though, and returned after the shift change to get another shrimp. He was a clever cat and was jokingly referred to by many as the Mayor of Royal Oak.

Mink also liked to jump into the back of pickup trucks to see what was inside. Well, once we got a call from a bar about two miles away at three o'clock in the morning saying that Mink had wandered in and made himself at home. Apparently, he'd been under a tarp in the back of someone's pickup truck, which had parked near our store. The truck owner drove to another city to visit his mother and when he stopped, Mink jumped out of the truck and walked into the bar. He liked women much more than men, so he'd been hopping up on the laps of the bar's female customers to get petted.

Mink was taken from us once. We didn't know it at the time, though. We thought he had simply run away. It turns out somebody saw Mink on the street and decided to take him home, despite the fact that he was wearing a collar and ID tag. We advertised to get him back and even offered a $100 reward. We never got any reports on him until, oddly enough, a contractor we do some work for happened to be working at a man's house several cities away. He called us to say that he was sure this guy had Mink. When the contractor questioned the man about why he was taking Mink's collar off, the man said the cat had some burrs. My son went over to the man's house, and sure enough it was Mink. The man refused to return Mink until we paid him the $100 reward money.

Mink was a little devil at times. When customers came in, Mink liked to go check out their cars. If there was a dog inside, Mink would jump up on the hood of the car and just glare at the dog, making it go nuts. Many times I had to excuse myself and go pull Mink off the hood of a customer's car. I can only wonder how many dashboards were ruined or coated with slobber because of Mink.

Sadly, Mink developed cancer and had three operations to try to save his life. In 1994, we did the only humane thing we could and had him put to sleep. Despite all he went through, he never complained. He was as friendly as ever and still made his usual rounds. To this day people still come in and ask to see Mink. We're catless now, but will always cherish the memories that Mink brought to us.

———————————————

Denny Dawes owns Howie Glass in Royal Oak, Michigan, which has been in business since 1912.

Although all cat games have their rules and rituals, these vary with the individual player. The cat, of course, never breaks a rule. If it does not follow precedent, that simply means it has created a new rule and it is up to you to learn it quickly if you want the game to continue.

—Sidney Denham

Big Tom, the Bacon Eater

Reba Dohanyos

I was eight years old in 1947 and my parents, four brothers and sisters, and I lived in a beautiful old farmhouse in a hollow in Colesburg, Tennessee, about forty miles southwest of Nashville. (Colesburg was small and doesn't exist anymore.) The land belonged to my grandparents, who lived above us on a hill. We had a strawberry patch, mulberry bushes, an orchard full of fruit trees, and a limestone-lined creek to swim in.

Times were hard back then, and we were poor by every definition of the word. We didn't have indoor plumbing or electricity at the time. We heated our home with a fireplace and a wood-burning stove in the winter, and kept our milk, butter, and other things cool in the freshwater spring in the summer. We also drew our drinking water from the spring year-round.

Although we didn't have much, we had a good time, and enjoyed playing with each other and our huge black tomcat, Tom. None of us was sure where Tom came from—he just seemed to appear one day. We think he may have belonged to our grandparents. He lived with us, though, and we all enjoyed him.

We didn't have a refrigerator or icebox at that time, and, as I said, we kept everything cool in the spring. My mother worked as a seamstress at the local shirt factory. One day after she got paid she went to the market to buy a pound of fresh bacon for dinner. All of us decided to go swimming in the afternoon, so my mother left the pound of bacon out on the kitchen table, thinking she would cook it when we returned. While we were in the creek having a good time cooling off, big Tom climbed up on the kitchen table and ate the whole pound of bacon—fat and all!

When we came home from swimming and my mother saw that Tom had eaten her bacon, she got so angry I thought she would burst! She grabbed the straw broom and chased him around the house, screaming the whole time. She finally caught him in the rear end with a solid whack and chased him outside. Poor Tom never did try to come back inside after that. And I'm sure he was quite sick for a few days after eating that much raw bacon.

About a year later my grandmother decided to sell all her land, which meant we had to move. We lived in a rented a house about a mile away. We moved everything we had, except Tom. My mother told me to go to the old farmhouse and bring him to the new place. Now, Tom had been raised totally on a farm, and he'd never seen a car before. I was holding him tightly in my arms walking along the two-lane blacktop highway that led back to our new home. Every time a car drove by Tom would get frightened and try to escape. I held on to him even tighter, and as a result, my arms got more scratched with each passing car. I cried all the way home, but I really loved Tom and didn't want him to get away.

Tom only stayed with us a short while at the new place. We were never sure if he went back to the old property, went off in search of a mate, or simply ran away. When we're remembering things at family gatherings now, we laugh at the "bacon incident"—but we wouldn't have dared laugh back then!

Reba Dohanyos is a homemaker who lives with her husband, Jerry,
in Warren, Michigan.

Cat Fact Quiz 2

Eating

TRUE OR FALSE
1. Cats should have tuna every day.
2. Five medium-size field mice is the same as a meal.
3. It's okay to give your cat chocolate.
4. Cats can taste sweets.
5. Cats won't eat what they can't smell.

ANSWERS
1. *False.* Tuna should be reserved as a treat because of its high mineral content.
2. *True.* The average cat-food meal is equivalent to five medium-size mice.
3. *False.* In fact, chocolate, Tylenol, avocado, poinsettia, lily-of-the-valley, and morning glory are all poisonous and sometimes fatal to cats.
4. *True.* Cats do have the ability to taste sweets.
5. *True.* If a cat can't smell its food, it won't eat. A cat has seventeen million nerve cells in its nose, which it uses to trace smells in its environment.

Losing the Kittens of My Youth

Claire Hinsberg

The neighbor's cat had recently given birth to a new brood of kittens, and after five weeks, I was offered the pick of the litter. There were seven of them—seven mewling little fur balls with pushed-in faces and mottled coats of calico, black, gold, and gray. One of the calico kittens was especially tiny, the runt of the litter. I zeroed in on him. "Ooo, that one's cute." I began to carefully scoop him up from his whimpering siblings, and he trembled and mewed piteously—the way only a frightened kitten undergoing separation anxiety can. It was then that I noticed his deformity. "My gosh! This kitten's only got three legs!"

I cradled him softly for a little while, and the trembling stopped. The kitten gave my hand a tentative sandpaper lick, and his little body began to vibrate with a faint whirring sound. "He's purring!" That settled it for me. I was eleven years old, tiny and runty myself, and tenderhearted. There was nothing I loved more than kittens. And this one *really* needed me. He was the smallest, the most vulnerable, the most in need of love. I took him home with me that afternoon and christened him Peppy Mewgoo, after a favorite rock star.

Over the next few months, Peppy seemed to thrive. Active and lively, he ran around playfully, batting at balls of foil and chasing imaginary mice on his three little legs—even climbing our carpeted stairs with aplomb. Our tripawed Peppy seemed happy and healthy and unaware that he was quadrupedally challenged. I was delighted.

Peppy was sweet natured and affectionate and would curl around my head when I went to sleep at night. Sometimes he would find my earlobe and start sucking on it, as if he was nursing. I figured maybe we'd taken him away from his mother too early, and his babyishness touched my little-girl's heart.

I showered Peppy with love and affection. But it turned out that this was not enough. There was something seriously wrong inside Peppy's kittenish little body—genetic development gone awry beyond just the obvious deformity of a missing limb. Peppy had internal problems, too, and they became more pronounced as the short months went by.

When Peppy was about four months old, I noticed that he struggled in his litter box, gamely trying to defecate but failing. It was as if his intestines were twisted. I became very concerned.

"There's something wrong with Peppy," I told my mom. She drove Peppy and me to the vet's. I could not know at the time that it would be my first brush with death.

The vet, a kindly soul, examined the kitty gently, delicately prodding Peppy's soft little belly with his fingertips. He sighed, then declared his diagnosis: "Well, your kitten is deformed on the inside, too. Internal birth defects. His intestines don't work the way they're supposed to, and there are probably other problems inside his abdomen, too, with his stomach and his digestion. It will just get worse for him. I think we're going to have to put him to sleep. . . ."

I began to cry and held Peppy up to my cheek. My tears left little round matted spots on the kitten's fleecy fur. As I petted him and kissed the fluff of his underbelly, a faint rumbling began. Peppy was purring like nobody's business. He was so helpless, so fragile, so damaged—yet so content. I loved Peppy, but I couldn't bear for him to suffer. My mother and I left the vet's alone that day.

I sobbed for three days straight and would not be consoled. Grief is perhaps childhood's toughest lesson—tougher even than learning to feel compassion for something smaller and more vulnerable than you are.

This was my first loss of a kitten. My second, while not involving death, would be just as heartbreaking as the first.

Connie was a beautiful creature, white and lithe and sleek, with striking green-blue eyes and a haughty carriage. She was the house-cat equivalent of a vamp—a real femme fatale. She'd disappear for days at a time, the local toms trailing in her wake, then suddenly reappear, hungry, bedraggled, and pregnant.

I'd had Connie since she was a tiny kitten, a surprise gift from my stepfather when I was twelve. One afternoon I'd come home from school and found this kitten, white as talcum powder, curled up on my pillow, gazing at me with almond-shaped turquoise eyes. I was so happy I cried, and she turned out to be the perfect antidote to my bereavement. I named her Consolation, dubbing her "Connie" for short.

Connie, an "outdoor cat," was a pleasure for the first five and a half months of her life. Mischievous, energetic, and independent, she alternated between frenzied bouts of prey stalking, playful tail chasing, and luxurious catnaps in a patch of sun. Slowly, her kittenish cuteness began to be replaced by a slinky feline pulchritude. She began to move with a sinuous grace, her haunches tensed, her head lowered, her wide eyes feral and predatory.

At six months, the tomcats took to Connie like catnip. I literally had to pry one of them—our big gold tomcat, Clem—off her with a kitchen broom when I caught the two *in flagrante delicto* in the family garage. After that, Connie seemed to be knocked up constantly.

She bore her first litter of kittens in the crawl space between the ceiling and the roof, above our downstairs bathroom. We discovered her kitten when a tiny white paw emerged, stabbing the air from between the vents of the bathroom-ceiling fan. My stepdad dutifully removed the fan's metal covering and retrieved four tiny kittens.

They were lovely—downy and golden and pink and white—befitting their mother's beauty, with the same bluish eyes and coiled-spring energy. Connie stuck by her kittens dutifully, nursing them, cleaning them, curtailing her nocturnal adventures for several weeks. (Subsequent litters would not fare so well.) The kittens were cute and easy to give away, so within about seven or eight weeks, Connie was on her own again. And loving it.

It was about this time that she must have made up her mind that kittens were a real drag. They whined and whimpered constantly, burrowing into her belly like rooting pigs after truffles. They cried and mewed and pooped, got soiled again as soon as she licked them clean, fought clumsily among themselves, and clung to her with a Velcro-like ferocity.

Connie abandoned her next litter. One day she was hugely pregnant, and she stole away, presumably to deliver. Two days later she came back, again svelte, without a single kitten in sight. No mewlings from the ceiling fan; no sudden stumblings across a hungry pile of slit-eyed puffballs; neither hide nor whisker to be seen. . . .

The toms began to prowl after her again, yowling with lust and frustration. Connie abandoned our family next. Ever selfish and autonomous, she probably caught the scent of some big sexy alley cat and deserted us for the lure of catnip for two and endless couplings.

Had Connie been a woman, she would've been the gorgeous, lissome model type: glossy, desirable, narcissistic, preening herself promiscuously before admiring toms, then toying carelessly with them—as if their hearts were mice—and leaving the drudgery of motherhood to plump, phlegmatic hauscats whose fondest wish in life was for a bowl of milk, a warm litter box, and a passel of squalling kittens.

Claire Hinsberg works as writer and editor of the *Record* and
Physician Update for Blue Cross, Blue Shield of Michigan and writes
short stories.

*A kitten is the delight of the household; all day long
a comedy is played out by an incomparable actor.*

—Champfleury

A Cat in the Beehive

Diane Cormier

I've heard of bees in the bonnet, flies in the ointment, and bats in the belfry, but never cats in the beehive. If I hadn't witnessed it myself, I wouldn't have believed it. And the story has nothing to do with bumblebees, stealing honey, or getting stung. No . . . it's more bizarre than that.

Our family had a few Siamese cats, and for me, a mere eight-year-old, they were fun to play with. Of course, I had other friends, but the cats were my buddies. All of the cats were nice, but one in particular was very affectionate and loved to have fun, play games, and make a lot of noise. In fact, all of our Siamese cats were rather loud.

This particular affectionate cat developed a habit of sleeping in people's hats. Whenever company came over, the cat would search out someone's hat that may have been left on a counter, crawl in, get comfortable, and claim it for his own. When it came time to retrieve the hat, the cat wouldn't get out! He'd hiss, howl, and scratch to keep his new possession. Many times people would have to wait for their hats until the next time they visited us or we visited them. People were afraid to challenge the cat for their hat.

Mind you, all this took place in 1972, when women were really experimenting with different hairstyles. Well, one day a friend of my parents came over for a visit. She had just come from the beauty parlor, where she had had her hair done up in a big blond beehive. I swear it stood eight inches off the top of her head and I remember giggling to myself when I saw it. She and my parents went into the kitchen to talk while us kids played in the living room. The two rooms were separated only by a half wall, so we could see and hear everything that went on.

My parents' friend sat with her back facing the living room, which meant that we could see the back of her head and the top of her "beehive" bobbing up and down as she talked. The cat didn't notice it at first, but soon he became mesmerized by this thing in the kitchen. He followed the bobbing hair with his eyes, and his tail began to twitch. Soon he got a little more curious and jumped up onto the counter. I could immediately see the horror in my father's eyes, but he pretended everything was normal.

The cat didn't do anything at first, just studied the foreign object on this lady's head. Then he slowly leaned over and began sniffing the bee-hive. I thought my father would burst into laughter or fright at any minute. The cat, satisfied with the smell of the copious amounts of spray holding the hairdo together, sat back and began licking his paws. I saw a small bit of relief in my father's eyes.

Then, without any warning at all, the cat leaped from the counter onto the lady's head and began batting wildly and ferociously at her bee-hive. The lady started screaming in terror, and hair was everywhere. I thought my father was going to have a heart attack. We watched in dis-belief from the living room. The whole thing only took about ten seconds, but it seemed like an eternity. The cat was finally pried from the lady's head. Her hair seemed to stick up and out everywhere, reminiscent of Medusa.

My father apologized profusely and graciously paid for her to get a new hairdo. She was actually quite nice about it and did visit us again. Of course, we hid the cats when she came over. This isn't the only crazed thing that cat did. He used to like to climb up the curtains, perch on the curtain rods, and wait for people to come through the door so he could jump on their heads. He wouldn't scratch or bite, but he definitely scared the daylights out of people.

How we lost the cat is even more hilarious. It seems he liked to hide in small places and especially liked to crawl into cars with open windows.

One warm day we had visitors from New York over, and they left their windows down. The cat crawled inside, and unbeknownst to the driver, got a free ride to New York! The minute the car stopped and the door opened, the cat jumped out and scampered away. That's the last anyone ever saw of him. Crazy cat!

Now that I'm grown and have a family of my own, I have two Bengal cats. They're good hunters and the wildest of all domesticated cats but they're pretty good with my children. One is an expert at catching hummingbirds in midflight.

Diane Cormier is a mechanical engineering consultant who lives with her two kids and two cats in Scottsdale, Arizona.

Way down deep, we're all motivated by the same urges.
Cats have the courage to live by them.

—Jim Davis

The Big Cats of Shambala

Tippi Hedren

When they hear me say that I am a big-cat lover, most people would get the impression that I'm some sort of eccentric who has a bunch of cats living with me at home. While it's true that I *am* a big-cat lover and *do* live with a bunch of cats, the emphasis certainly needs to be put on the word *big*—as in African lions, Bengal and Siberian tigers, cheetahs, servals, African and Asian leopards (spotted and black), and American cougars—more than seventy animals in all.

My fascination with big cats began in 1969 while I was in Zimbabwe filming *Satan's Harvest,* a movie in which I starred. One of my fellow cast members was a lion. His name was Dandylion, and he was a magnificent animal with an amber full mane. Until that day I had never been closer to a lion than circus seats, a zoo cage, or across a moat. During my childhood in Minnesota, and my teens in California, there had always been a dog or kitten around, and I'd ridden horses for both fun and film work, so I was an animal person. But it seemed to me that these huge beasts with gaping mouths, fangs larger than my thumb, and killer reputations belonged safely behind steel bars or in game preserves. That opinion was soon to change. To a degree.

During our stay in Africa, my then-husband Noel and I took advantage of occasional days off to travel to game preserves. It was our first trip to Africa and we didn't want to miss a thing. One day we found ourselves in Gorongosa, Mozambique's largest preserve, with elephants, lions, and thousands of other exotic creatures. We rented a car and followed one of the open-air tour buses through the park, finally drawing up in front of an abandoned flat-roofed Portuguese-style house. We overheard the bus guide say that the largest pride of lions in all Africa lived in the old house, formerly a game warden's residence until it was flooded out. Lions were all over the place. Some were on the roof gazing down on us, others were deep asleep in window frames, and two were comfortably seated on a dilapidated porch swing. It was quite a sight!

As we returned to our car and started out again, Noel commented that we should make a film about this. Movie people have a habit of making inane statements like that, but hardly any "ought-to-be-made" pictures are ever produced. Still, the thought of making a film with lions was intriguing. Noel and I talked excitedly about the idea all the way back to Zimbabwe. A chance encounter and an impromptu remark had stirred our imaginations.

Early the following year, Noel and I were back in Africa for another film, *Kingstreet's War,* and the proximity of the game preserves again stirred up that quirky idea of a cast of thirty lions. Those ideas and the fact that the wild animals were dwindling in number because of encroaching civilization, sport hunting, and poaching made our film even more important to us.

We began talking to as many lion handlers in Africa as we could. We knew that a film couldn't be made in Africa, because no trained lions existed anywhere between the Tropic of Cancer and Capetown. So the cats for our film would necessarily have to be amiable Dandylion types found in the United States.

We began searching throughout southern California for feline collectors and soon were involved in a whole network of big-cat people. Since lions who don't know each other will often fight because of genetic dictates, sometimes to the death, we decided that we would have to create our own pride of fifty homegrown lions. We learned of a man in Soledad Canyon with a lion named Neil whom we could safely hug and get to know. Once there, we struck up a friendship and explained what we wanted to do. He suggested that to really get to know anything about lions, we had to live with them for a while. Then he suggested that he bring Neil to our house for a visit! Neil became our first live-in lion.

Neil was a regular visitor at our house, usually coming at or just after sunset. We were told to hide our family dog and cat, because Neil might try to eat them. He made himself quite at home the very first visit. We inquired as to where we could get an adult lion of our own but were told that it would be easier and far less dangerous to bond with a cub. We searched, and within a few weeks a small, three-month-old cub named Casey became a permanent member of our household.

Soon we had another cub, then another cub, then another, and another . . . until our house started to look like some sort of illegal zoo! We knew they would all be eight or nine feet long (nose to tip of tail) and four or five hundred pounds in a few years, but we didn't deal with that fact because we were going to use them in the film and not have them live with us as pets. All we thought about was the day when we could begin shooting our film—with the willing cooperation of the full-grown cats we had raised from tiny cubs.

It was becoming increasingly obvious to all of us that, living with six growing lions, time was running out for us at our current home. The final edict came in January 1972, when an animal control officer politely but firmly told us to get the lions off our property within twenty-four hours. We called our friend in Soledad Canyon, who gladly agreed to board the animals for us. It was hard watching them go into confinement, but what other choice was there? For the next week I went out to Soledad Canyon every day to take them for walks by the river.

Then I had to leave for an extended trip with a group that feeds starving people in war-torn countries around the world. Three weeks into my journey, Noel called to summon me home for a film, *The Harrad Experiment*. A big surprise awaited me when I got there. Noel announced that he had purchased our friend's acreage in Soledad Canyon, adding that it made no sense to pay $25 per day, per animal, for boarding, and that the land would be perfect for our movie location.

No sooner had we erected a chain-link fence and started construction of some buildings on the compound, including a copy of the one in

Gorongosa, than more lions started to arrive. Most of them came from overcrowded animal parks and zoos, and from private citizens who had thought that big cats would make good pets but couldn't handle them. We quickly learned that it's not only animals in the wild who have a problem adapting, but also those in civilization. We eventually hired experienced workers and trainers to assist with everything that was going on at the compound.

Word had gotten out that we were accepting big cats and soon we were adding to the ever-growing lion pride on a weekly basis. Next came our first two tigers and after that an African bull elephant. We'd begun the slow process of turning the desert land into an oasis. Noel had begun to plant cottonwoods and bushes of the type we'd seen in Mozambique. Certain areas were being sodded. He had plans to further dam the little pond and turn it into a lake. The barren Soledad acres were beginning—just beginning—to look a little bit like Africa.

Throughout this period and for the next two years, while we were trying to raise money for the film, we had ample opportunity to think about the dangers, possibilities, and impossibilities of dealing with this bestial cast. It also gave us additional time to attempt a better understanding of big-cat behavior, especially their postures and language. Knowing these important things can sometimes mean the difference between life and death.

Financial backing finally in place, filming for *Roar* began on October 1, 1976. However, injuries and other setbacks shut production down for weeks at a time. Still we persisted. Then in the winter, two devastating floods within weeks of each other nearly wiped us out. Oddly enough, it gave us more motivation to complete our project. We resumed filming the following October. It wasn't until October 1979 that filming was actually completed, having used seventy-one lions, twenty-six tigers, ten cougars, nine black panthers, four leopards, two jaguars, one tigon, two elephants, six black swans, four Canada geese, seven flamingos, four cranes, two peacocks, and a marabou stork.

By 1983, our foreign sales of *Roar* were depleted in order to keep the animals. By that time we had fallen in love with the wild ones and it was unthinkable that they go somewhere else. It was also in 1983 that I started

Tippi Hedren and Arielle, an African serval
Photo by Bill Dow

the Roar Foundation so that monies could be donated to keep the animals. We became a sanctuary for rescued big cats. The Soledad site was renamed The Shambala Preserve. Shambala is a Sanskrit word meaning "a meeting place of peace and harmony for all beings, animal, and human." The Shambala Preserve is a nonprofit wildlife sanctuary that provides big-cat animal rescue services and education to children and adults through various outreach programs about the ever-present danger of extinction of these rare and magnificent creatures. Visitors to the site are given educational tours and a chance to visit up close with the animals. This place is a paradise for animals and the only game preserve of its kind in the United States.

I find a great sense of peace and enjoyment working with these animals. We are nationally recognized, with numerous states and various zoos throughout the country relying on the preserve to care for animals who have been abandoned or are in need of the unique environment provided at our eighty-acre site.

Tippi Hedren is an actress perhaps best remembered for her starring role in Alfred Hitchcock's *The Birds*. She is an avid believer in animal rights and continues her work at the Roar Foundation and The Shambala Preserve. Donations are accepted by the Roar Foundation at Box 189, Acton, California 93510, or by phone at 805-268-0380.

God made the cat in order that man might have the pleasure of caressing the lion.

—Fernand Mery

A Plea for a Cat

Anonymous

Would you care for me, as I care for my cat?
Oh, I know she is treacherous
    and her thoughts go no higher
Than mice and milk and a place by the fire;
She is getting old and fat
But when I sit alone in my evening chair,
I stroke her fur
I like to know she is there
    and to hear her purr.
Of course, you could not care for me
Like that!
I cannot purr as flatteringly as a cat.

The Way to a Woman's Heart . . . Is Through Her Cat!

Written slightly tongue-in-cheek by Glenda Moore

So you're dating a gal who shares her residence with a cat. If your relationship is going to get anywhere, I encourage you to follow each of these suggestions. (When I read these to a male friend and asked him if he thought any of them were funny, he said, "No, I think they are all perfectly accurate.")

- Never, ever mention that you can (or can't) smell the litter box.

- If the kitten wants to spend an hour untying your shoelace, let him. When he gets it untied, retie it so he can continue playing.

- Never make a big show of brushing the cat fur from your slacks.

- Get in the habit of putting a couple of sardines in your pocket—slip them to the cat when she isn't watching. (Note: You may have to do this through the entire dating period, because the cat will likely go for your pocket each time you visit.)

- Don't push the cat off the sofa if he's inserted himself between the two of you.

- If he's still sitting between the two of you when you get amorous, reassure him (mental telepathy is fine) that you have no harmful intentions against his companion, and move him gently to your lap. Try to keep one hand stroking the cat at all times in this situation.

- If you're spending the night, do yourself a favor and don't even *try* to sleep in the cat's favorite spot on the bed.

- When you phone her, ask about her cat.

- When she leaves the room to fix cocktails or check on dinner, ask her if she's got a cat toy handy so you can keep the cat entertained.

- If you're taking her out to dinner, ask her if it's okay to bring home a "cat bag" for the cat.

Glenda Moore works as an administrative assistant for the Utah Forest Service. She lives happily with her cats, Stanley, Galahad, Su-Su, Buster, Libby, MomCatII, DadCatII, and Low Rez, in Roy, Utah.

A cat allows you to sleep on the bed—on the edge.

—De Vries

The Spirit of Fizzbin

Gordon Allen

From June 1981 until June 1984, I lived on a floathouse (Alaskan for houseboat) on North Douglas Island, nine miles from Juneau, Alaska. The seven-hundred-square-foot house sat on the beach in the Mendenhall Game Refuge and had a spectacular view of jagged Alpine peaks, blue-hued glaciers, vast expanses of salt water, and towering cedars, many topped with a bald eagle. I bought the house with my then-girl-friend, Sheryl.

We both took to houseboat life, and even though the house sat dry most of the time, we enjoyed the rocking and swaying when the high tides floated our home. Although they were a bit unnerving at first, I gradually learned to sleep through the frequent storms and squalls of southeastern Alaska. We were isolated—we had no immediate neighbors, no phone (this was before cell phone days), no electricity, and no running water. This was quite different from my life in Seattle. Despite all of this, after a couple of weeks, we were well on our way to becoming tried and true boat folk.

We had one problem: mice. The previous owner had never warned us about *them*. They were all over, eating our food and scurrying about at will; they had come in under the doors and through just about any cracks that they could find. We had to do something—and fast!

We laid out our options: traps, poison, or a mouser. We jointly decided on a cat and the ever-resourceful Sheryl even knew of one looking for a home. We drove into town to meet a two-year-old cat named Fizzbin. Her owner was a *Star Trek* fan and named her after a card game from the show. We were pleased that the owner seemed nice and kind, and Fizzbin was just too good to be true.

Strikingly black and white in color and very furry, she was beautiful and even friendly. However, Fizzbin spent the whole ride home whining and cowering in the cat box. For two days she barely ate or drank and wouldn't go near us, hiding in every nook and cranny of her new home. "Cats hate to move," said Sheryl, "but she'll get over it."

After a few days, Fizzbin snuck out when a door opened, and she was gone. The mice were now gone, too, but we were completely devastated. We combed the neighboring woods and traipsed up steep game trails, but we could find no trace of our missing cat. As time passed, we kept hoping she would turn up. But we couldn't help but think about the area, with its bears, wolves, raccoons, and eagles—all of whom would kill a cat.

A month soon passed, and we went about our jobs and our chop-wood-carry-water lifestyle. The hummingbirds buzzing around our porch feeder were hardly a consolation. We wanted our cat back but quite feared the worst.

One day, Sheryl was riding her bike about two miles north of the house on the Douglas Highway. She heard a loud meowing, and who had shown up but Fizzbin! Thrilled, Sheryl rode home with the cat following her the whole way. Fizzbin soon swished into our house, and, at that moment, there was no hungrier, thirstier, or happier cat in the world.

Devouring cans of cat food and slurping lots of water, Fizzbin was now the prodigal cat, purring and eagerly being petted. We could see a total change in her overall demeanor and attitude. We could only imagine what Fizzbin's month-long wilderness epic must have been like, but we were pleased to see that we were being accepted by this now-grateful feline.

Sadly, Sheryl and I broke up that fall, but Fizzbin and I experienced and enjoyed the next two and a half years in that house. During the day, Fizzbin stayed outside and was somewhat feral. But at night, inside, she would sit on my lap and purr to her heart's content. That winter (1981–1982) was the most severe Juneau had seen in over forty years. One hundred and eight inches of snow fell in January. Fizzbin and I really bonded that winter as we both tried our best not to freeze to death.

The following summer I came very close to being evicted from my spot on the beach. Luckily, the Alaskan state trooper who had given me the order let me off with just moving the house closer to the shore. "You really shouldn't be here at all, but moving it closer will make it more legal," she said. "And by the way, I just love your cat," she added. Thanks, Fizz.

The following year I had a new girlfriend who moved in for six months. She brought music and home cooking to the floathouse, and good Colorado farm-girl energy. I think she was as crazy about Fizzbin as I was. During my last winter in Juneau, I was alone again, but as usual, Fizzbin was good company and really kept me going.

In the spring of 1984, I decided to move back to Seattle, which meant I had to sell the floathouse. Spring is usually a bright, breezy season in Juneau and the best time to sell a home in the normally rainy and dark state capital. On my last evening, I had everything moved out and was about to walk away for the last time to catch my ferry. I searched everywhere for Fizzbin but she was nowhere to be found. Sadly, I never got to say goodbye or pet her and hear her purr one last time.

I knew that the woman who had bought the house and would become Fizzbin's new owner was a fine person and would take good care of my cat. But tears were streaming down my face, and I knew why. I would miss the house and the view, but that was nothing compared to the pain I felt at leaving a good and loyal friend, Fizzbin.

Gordon Allen is a salesman who lives in New York City. Despite his current residence, he still considers himself an Alaskan.

The cat has too much spirit to have no heart.

—Ernest Menault
French writer

Maxwell Smart Meets the French Lady

Mitch Rosen

My mom gave me a kitten when I was thirteen, shortly after she and my father were divorced. I named him Maxwell Smart, after my favorite TV show character. He was an indoor-outdoor cat and became my best buddy and confidant throughout all of junior high and most of high school. We were inseparable, and he would always be waiting for me at the corner of my street when I walked home from school.

In my senior year of high school I went to live with my father, who despised cats. I was permitted to keep Maxwell, but he wasn't allowed in the house. He had to learn to be an outdoor cat from that point on. Well, across the street from my father lived a kindly, older French woman who had four cats of her own and who was the biggest cat fanatic I had ever met. She would cook fancy meals for cats, like liver pâté and other delicacies. She fell absolutely in love with Maxwell and took especially good care of him for me.

One day after I went to school, my dad, whom everybody in the neighborhood knew hated cats and had often heard him jokingly threaten them, went outside, got into his car, and started it up. Unbeknownst to him, Maxwell had crawled up in the garage and found a comfortable spot above the garage door. When my dad closed the garage door Maxwell somehow got squished and subsequently let out a horrific shriek so loud that Georgette, the French neighbor, heard it. My dad reopened the door; Maxwell came flying out and fled to her house.

About this time Georgette came running over and started screaming at my father, half in English, half in French, "You murderer! You cat killer! You tried to kill the cat!" My father tried to explain, but she wouldn't hear it. After that, Maxwell didn't spend too much time at our house. He survived, but I'm sure he used up one of his lives that day. I never saw Maxwell again after I went away to college.

The whole experience must have had some effect on my dad, though, because he has since become a cat lover and is now the proud owner of an indoor-outdoor cat named Maxine. He recently took in a stray cat who wandered over to his house, too. As for Georgette, she didn't speak to my father for a long time.

Mitch Rosen is president of Shared Marketing, L.L.C., a nationally known utility-based product and service provider in Redford, Michigan.

The purity of a person's heart can be quickly measured by how they regard cats.

—Anonymous

Cat Playhouse Fantasy

Bob Walker

I can *usually* resist the greatest of life's many temptations: chocolate, fine wines, ice cream. But when it comes to kittens and cats, those lovable little purring machines, I'm totally helpless. Yes, I am a cataholic, as is my wife (and best friend), Frances. Throughout our twenty-five feline-filled years of marriage, we have had more cats than many smaller neighborhoods.

It all began with Beauregard, a longhaired tabby we adopted on our wedding night. He was an affectionate, fun-loving cat who liked to entertain himself by climbing into our kitchen cupboard, spilling macaroni on the floor, and batting it all over the house. It didn't take long for us to figure out that Beauregard needed a playmate to diffuse his unbridled energy.

We answered a newspaper ad offering Siamese kittens and instantly fell in love with our second cat companion, Benjamin. Much to our delight, he and Beauregard became the best of friends. However, our insatiable urge to share our lives with cats didn't end there. Soon we had picked out another, and another, until our house had become a virtual wing of the local animal shelter. From the very beginning, Frances and I had decided that cats (instead of kids) would make up our family.

Rather auspiciously, in 1986, the Chinese Year of the Tiger, we moved into our present home near San Diego's sparkling Mission Bay. With a

The Cats' House © Bob Walker 1996

new house of our own, Frances and I were finally able to fulfill our family's needs. We had observed that felines have a natural inclination to climb, and truly love to look down on us. So we installed a floor-to-ceiling, rope-covered scratching post with a support beam wide enough for them to walk on. Our cats took to their new lofty playground right away. They would run full speed down our hallway, dash up the column, race across the support, and come to a screeching stop at the wall. There was nowhere else to go.

Literally, one thing led to the next. Adding a second entry exit was necessary to complete the loop so that our cats could avoid being cornered. We built a twenty-three-step spiral staircase to the seven-foot-high walkway. Now over one hundred feet of elevated paths extend throughout our house, allowing the cats to frolic above us. The catwalk has become our felines' favorite play area and sanctuary from children and other loud noises. Ruby red neon illuminates their zigzag path down the hallway through a fiery flame-shaped opening, enters our bedroom via a golden pyramid, travels by the Cats Only Clubhouse, and comes to a rest at their wall-to-wall inclined ramp.

TomCat, Jimmy, Jerry, Bernard, Denise, Frank, Molly, Louise, and Charlotte think all cats live this way. We think all cats should. By making public our private space, Frances and I hope others will be encouraged to create a better existence for their companions. Thankfully, our neighbors have been supportive of our cats' elevated lifestyle. We can't wait to see the looks on their faces when our feline fantasyland extends outside to the front yard!

Bob Walker and Frances Mooney currently have nine media-savvy cats. The couple's felines have been featured worldwide on film, print, and radio and are the subject of their own book, The Cats' House. *You can visit them on the Internet: http://www.thecatshouse.com*

*If there is one spot of sun spilling onto the floor,
a cat will find it and soak it up.*

—Joan Asper McIntosh

A Cat by Any Other Name (Would Still Be as Mischievous!)

Dawn Wells

I have the world's craziest cat, hence the title of this story. I rescued her from a neighbor's garage in Florida, where she was born. Her first name was Miss Match, because her right and left sides are completely different colors. A few days after I brought her home I renamed her Meow-Ing, because she wouldn't stop talking. She meowed all the time, carrying on her own conversation. This cat had a terrible dislike of walking on the floor and, instead, would jump from piece of furniture to piece of furniture, tabletops, chairs, whatever she could, to get around the house. That's when she got her permanent name, Ariel the Crazy Cat. (This is because she reminded me of an aerialist!)

When she was only months old, Ariel used to sneak out on to the balcony and climb up on the roof, which was three stories high. That in itself wasn't so terrible; after all, she is a cat. The problem was that the roof was slate and very slippery, and once she got up, she wouldn't or couldn't climb down. I certainly couldn't go up after her, so the first time it happened, I finally decided to go to my second-story landing to coax her to slide down into a laundry basket full of clothes. This became quite a ritual. Of course, there was always the danger of her missing the basket or me falling out the window! Thankfully, she's too old to do that anymore, and she spends a lot more time on the floor.

When I moved back to California a vet told me that it's always best

Dawn Wells and her thrice-named cat, Ariel

to keep cats indoors for a couple of weeks after a move so they become familiar with their new surroundings. Right after the movers left I looked for Ariel, but she was nowhere to be found. I thought for sure she had escaped when one of the doors was left open. About four hours later I was putting things away when I heard a faint mewing. At first, I couldn't figure out where it was coming from. As it turns out, she had crawled into the fireplace, jumped up to the damper, and accidentally shut the flue door. So she was trapped in the fireplace, and I was afraid to open the flue for fear of squashing her.

I called a few places that rescue animals, but they weren't available for many hours. Finally, a friend suggested I open the damper a little bit to see where she was. I looked up and there she was, hanging from the damper. It took a while, but I finally coaxed her out.

She was completely covered with soot, even in her eyes and teeth! By now it was 4:30 P.M. on a Saturday afternoon and I needed a vet or groomer. I found one who agreed to bathe her and check her out. It took four baths to remove all the soot. I recently returned to that same vet with Ariel and I noticed on her chart it said "NA." I said, "What does that mean?" The vet said, "That means 'Nasty Animal'! We have to wear gloves while treating your cat."

Crazy or not, I dearly love Ariel. I recently got a playmate for her and they seem to be doing fine. The new kitty, Driggs Mancuso, is a bit of a challenge for a fourteen-year-old sedate head of the household, but so far, so good. My little squirt gun helps with Driggs's discipline.

Dawn Wells is a veteran TV, screen, and stage actress, and is probably best remembered for her role as Mary Ann on the still-popular *Gilligan's Island* TV series. She has written a cookbook based on the series and currently produces and hosts *Reel Fishing,* a fishing show starring women.

When I play with my cat, who knows whether she isn't amusing herself with me more than I am with her?

—Montaigne

Mittens

Dolly Chaban

In 1932, my dad lost his job at Ford Motor Company in Rouge River—as did so many other fathers—and he decided to move his family of six, me being the youngest, out to a lovely country estate. Actually, it was kind of a dump—a swamp for woods, poor ground for growing, and a house without running water or electricity with a wood-burning stove in the center. You get the picture. But hey, it was the depression and we had a roof over our heads.

And what can keep the spirit of four little girls down? Not much. Into this cluster of people dropped a small bundle of fur with four little legs and four little feet, and each little foot had six toes. Six on each foot! This was a special kitten, to be sure. We named her Mittens in honor of her feet. She would romp and purr and tease and love in a special way like no other cat before or after. I was in awe of this kitten. Despite what was going on around me, life was perfect.

But into each garden some rain must fall. One day Mittens disappeared. No more romping, playing, purring, teasing, or cuddling—Mittens was gone! She left behind a silence so loud you could hear nothing else.

We girls slept upstairs in that old house around a large nickel circular vent in the floor. The night that Mittens left us, a somberness hung over us as we trooped up the stairs with hardly a word spoken. The ghastly night noises of an old frail house can be eerie and mournful to four imaginative girls. We heard sounds—creaks and rumbles and scampers and meows from far away—but we knew they weren't real. We finally slept. We awoke the next morning and traveled silently down to breakfast. Still no Mittens.

Sitting there eating our pancakes we could have sworn we heard meowing. But where was it coming from? We looked all over—in the corners, behind all the furniture, in the wood box, out in the lean-to shed, down in the always-flooded, unused cellar, but no Mittens. The sound always led to the wall. It didn't make sense. We followed that sound up the wall, up the wall, and even more up the wall. Sure enough, somehow she had gotten in the wall and there was no way out!

My dad and mom, both quick thinkers, knew they had to rescue the kitten before she died. I'm not sure how they did it, but they rescued Mittens without knocking any holes in the wall. Mittens was saved! With Mittens back and the family together, the farmhouse wasn't so bad and the world was truly a wonderful place.

Dolly Chaban lived on an apple orchard and farm with her family and various pets in Goodrich, Michigan, for a good part of her life.

For every house is incomplete without him, and a blessing is lacking in the spirit.

—Christopher Smart
British poet, referring to cats

Watson's Life of Luxury at the Feed Store

Rick Johnson

Growing up in the feed business was about as interesting as life could be, I suppose. There was always something new and different to do. The store started as Calvert Brothers Feed Store back in the early 1920s. It was sold to a Mr. Billings in the 1940s. That's where we came in: My father started working for Mr. Billings in 1948, and by 1959 he had bought the business from him. My father decided to keep the name, since everyone was used to calling it Billings Feed Store. I bought the business from Dad in 1985, a few years before he passed away. Because we added lawn equipment over thirty years ago, we renamed the business Billings Feed and Lawn Equipment.

One thing has remained the same throughout all the changes over the years: We have always had cats. We had cats in the store for obvious reasons—mice like feed and cats like mice. Two of the earliest cats I can remember are Smokey and Red. Smokey was a gray cat who lived to be about twenty-three years old. Red was sort of orange-red and lived about sixteen years. They were my constant pals as I grew up. This wasn't our first Smokey—there's always been a cat named Smokey living here. I'd say we're up to about Smokey VI by now.

Smokey and Red worked in tandem when it came to mice and dogs. Red would lie under the counter, and Smokey on top. One time a customer brought her dog in for some treats. She approached the counter and the dog started to get a little curious about Smokey, who was atop the counter.

Red, who was in his favorite spot underneath the counter, reached up with both paws and scratched the living daylights out of the dog. We immediately took both cats upstairs to get them out of sight. Unbeknownst to us, though, the cats somehow got out, ran around to the side of the store, and hid waiting for the dog. As soon as the dog appeared, they jumped him. We ended up having to pay for the dog's medical treatment.

Rick Johnson and Watson outside his store
Photo by Franklin Dohanyos

Red did the stranger things of the two cats. He loved to chase and catch small rabbits, birds, mice, or whatever and bring them into the store. He would jump up on top of the counter just as a customer was ready to pay and deposit a still-living yet somewhat gnarled creature, as a sort of gift. I think he liked to see customers go ballistic and see us struggle to catch the creature once he let it go.

For a while in the 1960s we sold canaries, which presented a risk considering the cats, but canaries were popular. One night the cats knocked all the cages down and ate all the canaries, about ten or twelve of them. My father was so furious, I thought he would strangle the two cats. We tried to sell hamsters for a while, too, but it didn't work out.

As the years went by, as with all living creatures, Red and Smokey passed on, but not the crazy cat antics. Our present cat is an eighteen-pound, black-and-white, shorthaired male named Watson. We got him about eleven years ago when he was nearly five years old. He came to us for adoption. We frequently place cats in good homes, and have for many years. Watson came in because his family was moving to Saskatchewan, Canada, which meant he would have to remain quarantined in a small cage for six months. They thought it was cruel to keep him in a cage that long, so they brought him to us for placement.

We let Watson run loose in the store to get used to the place, and he disappeared for five days. Apparently he was afraid and hid underneath the building. He was quite shy but we finally coaxed him out. He was a bit jumpy and had lost some weight. It didn't take long for him to gain it back and more, though. He eventually got up to twenty-three pounds. It wasn't that we were feeding him so much; it's just that every time he got hungry, he would go to the upstairs storeroom and rip open a bag of cat food. He'd have one flavor one day, another the next.

Over the years he's settled down some and has become somewhat of a legend here. When people come in they walk over to his favorite spot on the counter and give him a scratch behind the ear. About five years ago Watson became ill. The vet said one spot in his intestines had collapsed. They put a piece of plastic in its place, which worked fine for about six months. Then he began having more stomach problems and had to have the surgery all over again. Then, a couple of years ago, he began losing weight and always seemed to be thirsty. We thought, Now what? It turned out he had diabetes.

The diabetes has been rough on old Watson, considering he had an appetite like Garfield's. He was used to eating whatever we ate, at whatever time, including cake and chocolate milk. Now he gets daily insulin injections and a healthy diet of just cat food.

He is certainly a spoiled cat and has a routine that no one had better disturb. He greets me at the door each morning, comes up to the office and sits while I do bookwork, follows me downstairs and hops up on the counter for his injection, and then proceeds to howl until he gets a bowl of ice water. This happens every day without fail. Plus, his food bowl has to be filled to the very top or he won't eat.

Watson has always been a great cat. We've jokingly discussed having him stuffed and placing him on the counter. He moves so little now, no one would be able to tell the difference. He's very particular about where his litter box is. We normally keep it downstairs because there are only four steps for him to climb, versus more if he goes upstairs. We recently decided to finish off part of the downstairs for more floor space, though, and we had to move his litter box.

He came down to use his box, looked around a bit, then darted upstairs. I happened to be installing drywall right where his box is normally kept. He went upstairs to about the same spot where I was working below and proceeded to urinate. It seeped through the cracks in the old floor and dripped all over the drywall next to me, and I was using an electric saw at the time! We've learned to keep three or four cat boxes available at all times.

Many of our regular customers like to bring in their dogs, which we really don't mind. One time a customer brought in her Jack Russell terrier. This dog could jump three feet straight up in the air. I warned her not to let him near Watson, but she let him off his leash anyway. He saw Watson calmly sitting on the counter and immediately trotted over. As predicted, the dog got excited and began jumping up and down, up and down. Now, Watson's a pretty laid-back cat, but on about the twentieth time the dog jumped Watson reached out and smacked him in the head! Unfortunately for the dog, one of Watson's claws caught him in the side of the eye and we ended up getting sued. They had to perform laser surgery on the dog's eye to restore proper vision, which cost over $900.

These days there's a new Smokey in our feed store. He's about a year and a half old and has taken over all the mousing duties. Watson is getting old and slower and is happy to let his young apprentice do all the work. Smokey is very respectful of Watson's space and he, too, has learned a few times just how much aggravation Watson will take.

Rick Johnson owns Billings Feed and Lawn Equipment in Royal Oak, Michigan. Watson and Smokey are the best of friends.

How I Got My Very Own Zuzu Bailey

Karen Quinn

On December 12, 1994, I was trying desperately to get into the Christmas spirit. I hadn't shopped for a single present and had absolutely no desire to put up one inch of holly or tinsel. I knew I would be in big trouble if I didn't get in the ho-ho-ho mood soon, though, so I did the only surefire thing I knew of to revive my Christmas spirit. I popped in my *It's a Wonderful Life* video. Oh, sure, there was *Miracle on 34th Street* and *Rudolph the Red-Nosed Reindeer,* but I had a serious case of "bah humbug" and needed the ultimate fix.

About two-thirds of the way through the movie, I was completely filled with the warmth and memories of Christmas and my spirit was soaring, when the phone rang. It was my neighbor announcing that his cat had finally had kittens. I had promised him that I would find homes for all the kittens if he let me have the "pick of the litter."

When I arrived, five little newborn kittens were eating their first "lunch" with their mom proudly (and a little exhaustedly) looking on. I picked up each one to look at its face. When I got to the last one, the only one with tiger stripes, she let out the biggest mew I have ever heard. I put her little face up close to mine and said, "Relax, sweetheart, I'm your mommy." With that I reached out my hand to comfort her and my hand completely covered her face. I giggled and my neighbor wanted to know what was so funny. I explained that I had just watched the scene in *It's a*

Wonderful Life where Jimmy Stewart's character had reached out to comfort his daughter, Zuzu, and covered her entire face with his hand just like I was doing to the baby kitten.

"It's settled," I said, "her name is Zuzu." Five weeks later, Zuzu came home. Unfortunately, Zuzu had her first trip to the vet without me, because something had come up at work and I couldn't get away. My roommate, Diane Baeli (pronounced "Bailey") took her in for me and the receptionist at the vet's office mistakenly entered the name Zuzu Baeli. Upon reviewing the vet's statement I discovered the "error," but I never informed their office. Appropriately, she was meant to have the full name.

Thank you, Jimmy Stewart and Karolyn Grimes, for your part in naming my most precious pride and joy! (P.S.: I wouldn't be a very nice mommy if I didn't mention my other "furry children": Princess, Peanut, and Annie Girl.)

Zuzu and Karen celebrate Zuzu's first birthday.

Karen Quinn is an animal lover who lives in northern New Jersey.

Cats never strike a pose that isn't photogenic.

—Lillian Jackson Braun

A Birthday Present to Remember

Karolyn Grimes

Our house was much like *The Brady Bunch,* and then some. We were raising seven kids and always seemed to have two or three animals running around the place. We probably had a dozen cats over the years. We also had horses. A few of the kids eventually moved out on their own when they got older, leaving me to take care of whatever animals were left. I didn't mind too much because I've always loved animals.

Shortly before my birthday fourteen years ago, my son was driving to his apartment after work. It was a hot July day and his windows were down. He thought he noticed someone in the driver's seat of a truck ahead of him throw what looked to be an animal out the window. He pulled over to see what it was. At first he thought it was a rat, but then he realized it was a baby kitten, no bigger than his hand. He picked it up, brought it to my house, held out his hand, and said, "Happy birthday, Mom!"

I was stunned! Here was a practically newborn kitten in obvious distress, and he wanted me to accept it as a birthday present. Now, I don't mind receiving pets as birthday presents, but I prefer them to be healthy.

I told my son to take the kitten to a vet and see how much it would cost to treat him and find him a good home. He came back after a while

Karolyn Grimes with her favorite cat, Fritz

and said the cost was $100. I told him there was no way I was going to spend $100 on that kitten. It wasn't the hundred dollars so much as it was the principle of the thing. My son brings me a present that's going to cost me money? After a while I softened a bit and made a deal with him. I told him to take the kitten home for a week and care for him. If he survived, I would take him.

Miraculously, the kitten made it through the week. When my son brought him over, it happened that my regular vet was visiting to check on our horses. The vet examined the kitten and said treatment would cost $120. (It seemed the longer he lived, the more expensive he became.)

I was still against spending that much money on one kitten when I could buy a new one for $10, but one son offered to chip in $20, my daughter offered $20, the vet said he'd donate $20, and before I knew it, we easily had enough money to cover the kitten's surgery. The vet said the operation would be tricky because the kitten was so small, but he assured us he would do his best.

We brought him home after surgery and expected him to lie low for a week or so. Much to our surprise, the kitten was alert and playful and had a huge appetite. He grew up to be a monster-size cat and continues to eat us out of house and home. One of his favorite things to do is play in the sink with the water running. My son named him Fritz the Cat, after the cartoon movie of the same name. Although always a bit of a gremlin, he seems to be mellowing out in his older years. He's brought a lot of joy to my life and I'm very happy we kept him with us.

Karolyn Grimes is a former Hollywood child star, having been in such notable movies as *The Bishop's Wife* with Cary Grant and *Rio Grande* with John Wayne. She is perhaps best known for her role as Zuzu Bailey in the holiday classic *It's a Wonderful Life* with Jimmy Stewart. Karolyn lives in Kansas City with her two cats and a dog.

Cats seem to go on the principle that it never does any harm to ask for what you want.

—Joseph Wood Krutch

When Grandmother Crushed the Kitten

H. Ellen Whiteley, D.V.M.

My first job as a veterinarian was with Dr. Cashion, the owner of an enormous small-animal complex in Dallas. While I assisted Dr. Cashion at the central hospital, two other young veterinarians practiced at his outpatient clinics.

A short but dynamic man, Dr. Cashion had more stamina than any individual I'd ever met. His working day started at 7 A.M. and continued to 9 P.M., seven days a week. He knew all his clients by name and never appeared hurried. Each client received his undivided attention, and even if the waiting room was crowded, everyone was willing to wait his or her turn for Dr. Cashion rather than take a chance with that new female veterinarian (me).

In my first two days I was called upon to give just one nail trim and two vaccinations. Then, on Wednesday, while Dr. Cashion was at lunch, an emergency case came in. When I entered the exam room, I saw a large elderly woman clutching a tiny bundle wrapped in a towel. A small girl, wiping tears from her eyes with a tattered tissue, stood beside her. The woman gently placed the bundle on the table and turned to me. "Oh, doctor, I hope you can do something for our kitten," she said. "I tripped and stepped on her while she was playing in the kitchen."

I felt a moment of panic as I looked at the kitten, a plump, two-month-old calico. She lay prone on the table with her neck stretched back and all four legs rigidly extended. The kitten was cold, obviously in shock. Cradling her in my hands, I rushed into the treatment room, where I gave her an injection that I hoped would raise her blood pressure and then started her on intravenous fluids.

I turned to the woman and the girl, who had followed me into the treatment room. "She's in bad shape," I said. "We'll first try to treat her for shock, and if she makes it through that, we'll try to determine whether she has permanent nerve damage."

Placing a hand on the girl's shoulder, the woman replied, "I'm Mrs. Murphy and this is my granddaughter Ruth. The kitten belongs to her, and I feel just awful about stepping on her. Please do whatever you can." As they turned to leave, the girl said, "Her name is Pumpkin," and began crying. I wished that I could say something comforting, but I didn't have much hope for little Pumpkin.

I inserted an oxygen hose into a plastic bag to make a small oxygen tent and placed the kitten into it. When Dr. Cashion returned, he peered in the door with the comment, "That kitten is hopeless; you ought to put her to sleep." But I continued to work with Pumpkin during the afternoon. She was my only patient, and Dr. Cashion was too busy to find other things for me to do. As I left for home that evening, I feared the kitten would be dead the next day.

Later that night in bed, I worried that I hadn't done everything possible for Pumpkin. I worried that Dr. Cashion was right—Pumpkin would remain paralyzed and should have been put to sleep. But the next morning she was alive and for two days seemed to slowly improve.

Friday, I was encouraged to see her looking alert, her legs no longer stretched out stiffly in front of her. That day Dr. Cashion entered the ward and said, "Mrs. Murphy called to ask about the kitten, so I told her that she has permanent brain damage and should be put out of her misery. She agreed but wants to talk to you first."

I was shocked and disappointed. I knew Dr. Cashion wasn't heartless; after years of observing similar cases, he simply felt the kitten would never fully recover. As I looked down at Pumpkin, I began a debate with myself. If I were to dismiss Dr. Cashion's advice and ask Mrs. Murphy to give us a little more time, would I be building up her hopes and her veterinary bill only to return to her a permanently damaged kitten? Reluctantly, I moved toward the telephone. I was uncertain what I would say. Ruth answered the telephone.

"This is Dr. Whiteley," I said. "May I please speak with your grandmother?"

"It's about Pumpkin, isn't it?" she asked. "Dr. Cashion said that she should be put to sleep." The soft sniffling came over the telephone.

"Your grandmother and I will try to decide what is best," I said with a lump in my throat.

Mrs. Murphy came to the telephone. "What do you think?" she asked. "You've been Pumpkin's doctor from the beginning, and we'd like to know what you think we should do."

I felt a warm glow. Someone had faith in me—regarded me as a real doctor. "Mrs. Murphy, Pumpkin's a long way from being fully recovered," I said, "but I feel we still have a chance. She has improved slightly with each day. She doesn't appear to be in pain, so if it's all right with you, let's give her a few more days."

"Oh, I'm glad you feel that way," she said. "If there's any hope, I want to keep trying."

During the weekend, Pumpkin improved even more. She started eating baby food without assistance, so on Monday I was able to release her to the care of Mrs. Murphy. At the end of the week, she called me to say that Pumpkin was doing very well, although the kitten could still not walk or stand unaided.

That was the last time I heard from Mrs. Murphy. In the meantime, things were changing for me. A young veterinarian employed at one of the outpatient clinics quit to start his own practice, and I took his place. I began seeing more patients, and, busy with the routine of examinations and surgery, I forgot all about Pumpkin and her trauma.

Then about six months later, a woman entered the clinic. In her arms she carried a beautiful, sleek calico cat.

"You don't recognize us, do you?" she said. "This is Pumpkin."

I was astonished. The cat was perfect in every way. She showed no signs of the accident.

All this happened twenty-five years ago, but the lesson it taught me has served me many times in the years since. As I think about the case now, I realize that Pumpkin's nervous system had not sustained permanent damage. Today, treatments for such cases are certainly much more advanced, and there is even the likelihood of recovery. However, doctors see so many cases that we begin to feel confident in our ability to make a prognosis. We know what technology can do and what it can't. Pumpkin's case continues to impress upon me that every patient is an individual and each case is different. God is the healer, and we are mere token instruments of that healing. Perhaps He heard a little girl's prayer for Pumpkin.

H. Ellen Whiteley is a veterinarian and noted author and writer of books and articles in the veterinary field. She continues to contribute articles to the *Saturday Evening Post,* including Pumpkin's story.

The smallest feline is a masterpiece.

—Leonardo da Vinci

An Old Russian Prayer for Animals

Anonymous

Hear our prayer, Lord, for all animals,
May they be well-fed and well-trained and happy;
Protect them from hunger and fear and suffering;
And, we pray, protect especially, dear Lord,
The little cat who is the companion of our home,
Keep her safe as she goes abroad,
And bring her back to comfort us.

Saying Goodbye to Higgins

Teresa Casella

To us, cats are companions, but to the ancient Egyptians, they were gods. Higgins believed the ancient Egyptians had the right idea. He would always look at you as if to say, "I'm Higgins . . . you're not." Higgins was by far the most intelligent cat I have ever come across. He was a Manx and weighed twenty-five pounds at his heaviest. He hated the idea of losing weight! We tried a couple of diets on him but they stressed him to the point where he felt the need to keep me up all night until I fed him.

We fought a bit when I first got him, until he had me fully trained. He was about seven years old when we got him and we had him for about twelve years. He was very much a people cat and very much a part of our family. He loved car rides and searching for critters in the strawberry patch. He also loved getting up on the windowsill and jumping (all twenty-five pounds) onto my chest when I was sleeping and his food dish was less than half full. I woke many mornings as early as 3 A.M. to the sound of cupboard doors opening and then slamming shut. Usually, it was the cupboard that led to his food.

One night I put my then-five-year-old son to bed, shut his door, turned up the stereo, and started cleaning house. About an hour later, I heard a bloodcurdling scream. My first instinct, of course, was to go check on Tim. I raced to his room and threw open the door, only to find him still fast asleep. I checked for a pulse, then make a quick scan to be sure there was no blood.

Another scream. I turned the music down and listened for more. Silence. Then finally, another scream. I don't know if you have ever heard a Persian scream, but it's scary and loud! I headed for the noise only to find little Diamond Lil, my Persian cat, under the desk with Higgins hovering over her, just staring. Her heart was racing and it took a while to calm her down. Higgins simply walked away like he just couldn't understand what the problem was. He liked to harass the other cats. He never beat them up, though. He would simply give intimidating glares and march to the music of *Jaws,* and the other cats would run. With humans, however, he loved to snuggle, and no matter what your day had been like he would cheer you up.

Higgins developed feline infectious peritonitis and a tumor in his thyroid two years before he died. But he was a fighter and did okay with it. Then suddenly, he developed tumors in the pit of his stomach and was having a pretty difficult time. Higgins died July 18, 1994, from complications of old age and his various ailments. My son Tim made a headstone and we buried him in his favorite place, the strawberry patch. There will never be another Higgins. He will always be missed.

Teresa Casella is a secretary for the state of Idaho. She lives in Idaho Falls with her two sons, Chris and Timothy, and her two cats, Tas and Sasha.

In ancient times, cats were worshiped as gods;
they have never forgotten this.

—Anonymous

Newton, Last of the Small-Game Hunter-Gatherers

Teresa Bloomers

Our cat, Mr. Newton, is a big charmer and comes up with many new surprises all the time. We live on a creek, and every fall we have salmon spawning. Last fall, I was sitting at the computer as I often do, and Newton came in, as he often does, to check in with lots to say. He is *very* interactive and sometimes can even get one of us to actually come out and walk to the creek with him.

Anyway, I was at the computer and I heard him come through the swinging cat door like always, with much to say, rubbing against my leg and talking. I was very busy so I kept on typing, stopping occasionally to reach down and pet him or talk back to him. I decided to stretch my legs while still sitting there—when my feet touched something cold and wet. I looked down to find a salmon head at my feet, and a very proud Mr. Newton looking up at me. His breath even smelled like fish. I picked up the salmon carcass and started to walk to the creek with it, when he ran zooming by, trying to cut me off and get his salmon back. I tossed it in the creek, but I guess it didn't go far enough, because he snatched it back out. I finally just had to wrap it in newspaper and toss it out. So now every fall (without his fishing license . . . shhh) Newton is busy trying to fish in our creek.

Most of the time he likes to bring his catch in alive. A while ago he brought in a mole and let it loose in the house. It took *all* afternoon to get to that little thing. Newton got bored with the mole getting stuck between the books on the bookshelves, and left me to hunt it down. He did come in to check up on me, played a bit, and we finally got the little mole to scoot across the room. I opened the door and out it went, with Newton not far behind.

I have never had a cat quite like Mr. Newton. He's more like a puppy dog, a man's best friend. He always has to be around us to see what's going on and give you that "what ya doing" look.

He follows us all around the yard and likes to eat chicken feed and waterfowl feed. No wonder he has a shiny, waterproof coat! It's never a dull moment with Mr. Newton!

Teresa Bloomers owns a Web page and desktop publishing business in Washington State. She lives with her husband, two cats, three geese, six hens, three doves, and two finches in Issaquah.

There is nothing in the animal world, to my mind,
more delightful than grown cats at play.
They are so swift and light and graceful, so subtle
and designing, and yet so richly comical.

—Monica Edwards

Cat Fact Quiz 3

History

TRUE OR FALSE
1. In ancient Egypt, cats were killed as part of worship rituals.
2. Cats were praised all over Europe in the Middle Ages.
3. The first cat show ever was held in London.
4. Scientists have identified more than two hundred distinct breeds of cats.
5. People in Great Britain believe black cats bring good luck.

ANSWERS
1. *False.* In ancient Egypt, killing a cat was a crime punishable by death.
2. *False.* In fact, during the Festival of St. John, in the Middle Ages, cats were burned alive in town squares.
3. *True.* The first cat show ever was at the Crystal Palace in London in 1871.
4. *False.* Only about a hundred distinct breeds of the domestic cat have been identified.
5. *True.* Black cats have been believed to bring good luck in Great Britain for many years.

My Kingdom for a Pen

Maureen Bond

When I first met Larry, my former husband, he owned two cats, Stevie and Herman. I was very allergic to cats, but I really wanted to be with Larry. I was able to salvage the situation by limiting my contact with the cats and keeping a good supply of allergy pills on hand. It all worked out for the best, as we got married and the four of us lived together in a beautiful home.

These cats were my husband's babies. They greeted him at the door when he came home from work and occupied all of his couch time. He always spoke so kindly to them; his voice would change, as if he was speaking to an infant. As for me, I've never been a big cat fancier, but Stevie and Herman seemed to grow on me the longer we lived together. I soon learned that Herman was the character of the pair. Often one of them would come into my home office for a scratch or to get petted. Herman, however, wanted more. He was extremely curious and would jump up on my desk, I suppose to see what was going on near my computer.

Herman invented a little game that he liked to play. If I was out of the office for any reason and he was in the vicinity, he would jump up on my desk and steal pens. I could always tell when he had stolen one because he had a different kind of meow. It was louder than usual and went on forever. It's as if he wanted me to find him and his ill-gotten swag. First he would steal the pen. Then he would go to a different part of the house, announce that he had my pen by dropping it on the hardwood floor, and begin meowing. This went on time after time.

One day I had a meeting at my office with a client. I needed to write something down, but my pen—in fact, all of my pens—was missing! I excused myself and went searching for Herman. Sure enough, at his feet was a collection of various-colored pens. I would have laughed out loud had a new client not been in my office. Herman made me laugh out loud on more than one occasion, except the time he urinated in the dryer—but that's another story!

Maureen Bond is a graphic designer and graphic artist who lives in Oakland County, Michigan.

Cats are intended to teach us that not everything in nature has a function.

—Garrison Keillor
humorist and writer

Symphonic Metamorphosis on a Theme of Tuna

Jurgen Gothe

I've enjoyed cats for as long as I can remember. So much so that at one point we had five of them living with us. Currently, we're down to just one: an eighteen-year-old Manx named Herbie. True to the Manx's reputation, Herbie is loud and thinks he runs the household. And, like myself, he enjoys well-prepared food. He also enjoys traveling to the radio station to watch me while I host my daily classical and jazz variety show.

I'll never forget my first interview, not merely because of the significance of it being my first, but because it was an interview with none other than Morris the Cat. He decided he wasn't going make any noise whatsoever that particular day, so we had to turn up the gain on the microphone to hear him purring. It drove the studio engineers crazy, but we got our interview. The following is one of my favorite humorous cat stories that I have written, which I hope you will like as well.

The domestic cat's role in the development of music has generally been overlooked by musicologists. Tending to dismiss such compositions as "The Cat's Fugue" as indulgent curiosities has done little to secure for these talented furry creatures a permanent position in *Grove's*.

How many people, for instance, know about the all-cat orchestra of Mannheim? At the beginning of the seventeenth century, when the musical expression of the day was filled with flourish and embellishment, sev-

*Jurgen Gothe with his first ever in-studio interview,
Morris the Cat*

eral cats took it upon themselves to counter these excesses with a return to simple, direct melodic development. The all-cat orchestra was formed in Mannheim as a result and received an annual stipend from both the German and the Austrian royalty, who were vying with one another for the favors of the ensemble. The segregationist policies of the group did give rise to controversy, and shortly thereafter a splinter group was born, augmenting the ranks of the felines with roosters, dogs, and the like. Since there was little demand for the aberrant group in Mannheim, they relocated to Bremen, where they enjoyed considerable public acclaim and got a recording contract.

According to Slonimsky, many famous composers have been accused of making cat sounds in their music. Bizet and Liszt, Chopin and Strauss, and, of course, Wagner, Varèse, and Schoenberg, all came under attack. However, in their own music, on which precious little scholarly comment exists, the cats have retaliated by utilizing composers' names in their own particular form of invective.

Orange Julius, one of the leading feline writers of the time, claimed that a performance of the "Symphonic Metamorphosis on a Theme of Tuna" had all the elegance of "Liszt in Heat," apparently a frequent occurrence for that particular composer. Later, "Kitten on the Keys" was dismissed as being the "product of an immature mind, not unlike Beethoven with a headache chasing field mice."

History is generally silent on the subject of Bach's cat. Not only did the great composer father an inordinate number of children, but he also carried a large tabby around with him in a bread basket all through Leipzig. (In all fairness it should be pointed out that while Bach had a cat, he also had a duck and a six-pack of gerbils.)

There is no doubt that Bach was one of the greatest of all composers, but it is also worth noting that he was an extraordinarily talented cat trainer. Each morning he would give his cat a few guilders or gold crowns and send him off to the corner to buy a paper. The cat sometimes squandered the money on jujubes and didn't return until spring. But most of the time by noon or one o'clock, Bach could be observed sitting on the porch with a Cuba Libre, reading through the Hapsburgs' gossip column, and trying to make sense out of the by-then-tattered stock-market quotations.

Bach's cat also played excellent canasta, learned to serve champagne in a restaurant, and, later in life, dabbled in neurosurgery. But perhaps the most amazing achievement of this animal was that Bach had taught him to make spaetzle. So on a Friday night, after a hard day of writing fugues, Bach would call over a couple of friends to while away the evening. I remember dropping in one night. I'd sold him a used clavichord that summer, and we had become friends.

I walked in the kitchen and there, to my surprise, was Bach's cat, his arms covered in flour, rolling spaetzle on a wooden board. The cat took my coat and wig, got me comfortable in the den, poured me a hefty daiquiri, and said that Bach would be down shortly. I could hear the master upstairs, finishing off BWV 656. Anna Magdalena was quilting a large tea cozy by the fire, and a couple of boys were playing on the floor. Carl Philipp Emanuel wanted to borrow the virginal for a date, and Anna Magdalena gave him the keys and told him to have it home by ten.

I lit a cigar. The cat came in from the kitchen, stoked the fire, and offered a tray of shortbread. The spaetzle, he said, would be ready in about an hour.

Bach came down the stairs all hearty and full of good humor because he'd cleared Sunday's cantata out of the way. We discussed politics and

Rhine vintages and got pretty jolly over a bottle of Siebenzwergenthaler Spätlese.

Around eight-thirty the cat announced dinner, and we sat down to spaetzle, wild mushrooms, venison, and a terrific dessert, the recipe for which I forgot to ask. I left around midnight; the stars were out and the night was warm, so I walked home.

I'll never forget turning to wave. There in the doorway stood the greatest composer of all time, his family, and a cat that could make spaetzle, waving back.

Jurgen Gothe is an internationally known food and wine critic and writer, and host of CBC Radio's Disc Drive, *based in Vancouver, B.C., Canada.*

There are two means of refuge from the miseries of life: music and cats.

—Albert Schweitzer

My cat does not talk as respectfully to me as I do to her.

—Colette

Kitty Kat Believe It or Nots

Stephen Gardea

- Rolled-up toilet paper is a magnet to kitty feet and it takes a long time for them to break their paws free.

- Cats can see ghosts and invisible creatures.

- Oriental shorthairs think they can drink all the water out of a fishbowl and then eat the goldfish.

- Dogs come when you call; cats have answering machines.

- There is no snooze button on a cat who wants breakfast.

- The more money you spend on a cat toy, the less the cat will play with it.

- Two cats can shred an ordinary houseplant in three minutes or less.

- No matter where you lost that newspaper rubber band, your cat will find it, eat it, and barf it up on the newest piece of furniture you own.

- A cat will shed every hair on its body within a year.

- No matter how mad a Manx will get, it will never bush up its tail.

- Siamese or Orientals curled up together will produce enough heat to make a waterbed boil.

- Siamese cats actually think before they do something clumsy.

- Cats really can understand what you are saying, but choose to ignore you.

- Oriental cats' diets are made up of socks and undergarments.

- Manx cats really have brains.

- Wherever you leave your Persian cat in the morning, you'll find it there when you get home after work.

- You will find cat hair on everything you eat, even when you eat out.

- You will never have a matching set of earrings for longer than a month.

- No matter how late in life, a cat can still train a human.

- Cats don't always land on their feet after falling asleep on top of the TV.

Stephen Gardea works for the city of Boulder, Colorado, and lives on a farm in Erie, Colorado. He has been active in the Cat Fanciers' Association for ten years, showing and breeding regional-award–winning Abyssinians and Ocicats, and hopes very soon to be a CFA judge.

The Cat Who Wouldn't Die

Doug Stych

I once had a cat living with me whose name was Deckerd. He was an all-black, longhaired, neutered male with a pugnacious attitude. He would stalk and attack all other cats, no matter what the circumstances, usually getting thrashed for his troubles, because his size was in no way comparable to his demeanor.

When Deckerd was about five years old, much past his fighting prime, I noticed that his face had been injured, in fact bitten pretty badly. The resulting infection was rather unpleasant, to say the least. He was taken to the local vet for the usual treatment for abscesses, which entailed anesthesia and a good cleanup of the wound. Deckerd was no stranger to this treatment and no problems were anticipated.

I dropped him off at the vet in the morning and went to work, which was only a block away. That afternoon I got a call from the veterinarian, who sadly informed me that Deckerd died during the operation. I was understandably surprised and asked what had happened. The vet replied that Deckerd had stopped breathing after the anesthetic was applied. He was revived, but stopped breathing again shortly thereafter. They revived him a second time, but again, he stopped breathing. After heroic efforts, the vet and assistants decided that nothing else could be done.

Then something miraculous happened. Shortly before the end of the vet's phone call, just as I was making arrangements to pick up the body,

Deckerd the cat at home in California

the vet said, "Wait just a second, someone is yelling at me." I could hear the muffled sounds of people talking excitedly. After a few moments the vet told me, "An assistant was able to get Deckerd breathing again; perhaps you should come over here."

Of course, I wasted no time in rushing right over to the vet's office. Upon arrival, I went to see the poor kitty. He was lying on a table with an IV needle in his leg and a tube in his throat to help him breathe (sort of a miniature kitty iron lung). He looked very flaccid, but even unconscious he was definitely alive. The vet wasn't very confident about his chances, since he had been revived three times. Even if he did survive, she thought there was a very good chance that he had suffered permanent brain damage.

Well, I decided, if he wanted to live that badly, he should have a chance. That night he was transported to a twenty-four-hour-care facility where his condition could be monitored. By evening he was just barely conscious and unable to move. I left instructions that he should not be revived in the event his life signs failed again. By this time the anesthetic had worn off, and if his breathing stopped again it would be a sure sign that he had suffered terrible brain damage.

In the morning, however, he looked a little better and he was transported back to the vet's for further care. He spent the next five days there, slowly recovering his strength. I went by to visit him whenever I could, and despite the fact that he couldn't walk or see, he seemed to recognize me and gave me every indication of wanting to stick around.

I brought him home, weak and barely able to stand. He was completely blind, but his happiness at being in familiar surroundings was incredibly heartwarming to see. While he was supposed to be kept indoors, he nonetheless insisted on going outside. He would painfully make his way to his favorite tree and sit with a look of sheer contentment. I was worried about him and kept a watchful eye on him through the window. After a few hours he disappeared. I searched and found him lying in some tall weeds and grass by the side of the yard. He had fallen over and was lying there with all four feet in the air, looking very puzzled. I uprighted him and he went back to his tree.

Over the weeks that followed, his condition slowly improved. He was walking better and eventually regained essentially all his coordination. After some time his eyesight returned, though not without a lot of misjudgments during the recovery period. Perhaps the most remarkable thing of all is that his attitude toward other cats appears to have permanently changed—now he likes them! My theory is that since he couldn't see them while he was blind, he more or less decided they didn't exist. Or possibly he is just happy to be alive.

Doug Stych works as a contractor and handyman when not rescuing distressed cats. He and Deckerd live in El Sobrante, California.

The Nature of Things

Jean Dohanyos

It couldn't be just any kitten—it had to be a special one, I decided. I was in kindergarten or so, and my family was visiting my grandparents in the country—as we did every Saturday—and one of Grandma's farm cats had had kittens. Tiny, cuddly little scraps of fur making itty-bitty mewing sounds, and Grandma, who was a very wise woman, did not let us touch the kittens for ever so long because she said the mama cat might reject her babies if we got our smell on them. When we first saw them, we thought they didn't look much like cats—their heads were so big and their eyes were not yet open. And then Grandma had to tell us that if we went to the mama cat's home too much the tabby would move the kittens, and that wasn't a good idea. So we had to be patient and wait until the kittens got to be big, like us. And at last the time had come to choose one for our very own.

Now, this was a little tricky, since our mother and father had told us we would not be taking anything home, but grandmas have a way of working things out and our grandma was very wise indeed. So there we sat, my big sister and I, with our feet pressed together to make a diamond-shaped pen in the green spring grass, and the kittens tumbled and romped inside our boundaries as if to show us they had gotten the hang of legs after all and we weren't so much older than them as we thought.

As I remember, there was an assortment of colors to choose from, tortoiseshells and rust orange, but my sister immediately selected the pure white one and said, "This one's mine and I'm going to call her Vanilla Valentine." Now, this was a problem, because she was the only all-white cat, which made her special, and because that name was a most remarkable name. How do you top a name that so beautifully rolls off your lips and so perfectly describes a most adorable kitten?

Well, I was determined to rise to the challenge. I would find a cat who was more special than the white one and just as significant as I was. (I knew I was special because my sister, Karen, had to share her name with several other Karens I had met, but I was the only Jean I knew of, so that proved it: I was unique.) I watched the little fur balls intently and then announced my decision. "I will take this one."

I had selected the only all-black kitten in the litter for two reasons: First, he was not white, and second, he had special powers. I knew this to be true because I had seen tagboard cutouts of black cats in school, and they were perched on the ends of witches' brooms or howling at paper pumpkins. And everyone knew that terrible things could befall you if a black cat crossed your path. So this was clear evidence that black cats had the power of mystery, an irrefutable indicator of specialness.

Yes, this was the cat. Now to conjure up a name . . . I was wracking my five-year-old brain for a name with appropriate impact when Grandma spoke to me gently, in her wise way. "Now, honey, you should choose a different one—this one is a tom, and tomcats are born to roam."

In those days, I recall, I was filled with self-assurance, and while I appreciated Grandma's advice, I was convinced that this cat would discover my uniqueness and thus realize that nothing could be more wonderful than staying put with me.

"No. I want *this* one," I stubbornly insisted. "He is the only one who fits his name: T. J. Whatchamacallit." There! I had trumped Karen's nomenclature, even if it didn't have quite the same ring to it. I went on to explain that the *T* stood for Thomas, the *J* for Jean (since his owner's name was Jean), and *Whatchamacallit* for a word that had come from my father's lips with just the right hint of whimsy.

And so the little kittens became our first pets. Vanilla Valentine grew to be a lovely, even-tempered cat, as appealing as her name, which was shortened to just VV. T. J. grew into his mystique, even if his name relapsed into just plain Tommy. And as he grew, my grandma would remind me when she came to visit, "Don't be disappointed if he runs away, honey. Tomcats are born to roam."

Outwardly I maintained my position of respectful disagreement. But inwardly I was troubled. Grandma knew many things. Could it be that Tommy would actually desert me? I must have made my misgivings known to my mother, because my parents spent precious dollars to have the dear boy neutered. But it was to no avail. T. J. had caught a whiff of the alley's allure at the end of our block, and it wasn't long after the operation that he decided to strike out in search of adventure. I was heartbroken . . . or peeved . . . or perhaps a bit of both. How could this have happened? How could it be that my superior cat, with his superior name, had vamoosed, while Vanilla Valentine was still here to purr away my sister's blues?

Grandma knew the pain in my heart and sought to give comfort. "Honey, a tom just has to roam. It's his nature, and you can't expect him to go against his nature."

Well, I knew T. J. would come back to me. After all, was he not special? Was I not special? Did we not belong together? (Didn't he value his relationship with VV?) When I remembered to be heartbroken, I was. And when I forgot, I found other activities to fill my days, until one bright afternoon I had come out of our back door, into the driveway, and stood face to face with a black cat making a most peculiar yowl. He was gaunt, his coat was not as impeccably shiny as it had been, but the realization that Whatchamacallit had returned hit me like a tidal wave.

I rose to the occasion with a melodramatic welcome: I burst into tears and began sobbing my cat's name over and over as I tried to approach: "Tommy! Tommy! *Tommy!*"

This lack of decorum seemed to render him nonplussed. I think back now and believe that he had presented himself to do two things: He wished to assure me that he was all right, and he knew he needed to say goodbye. Tommy had outstripped me, growing beyond my child's play, and now had little patience for silly maudlin outbursts. He yearned to return to a world I would not meet for at least a decade. With a final twitch of his ear and a flick of his tail, he turned and melted into the bushes, never to be seen by me again.

Grandma, of course, was right, as grandmas inevitably are, and I realize she was trying to teach me a valuable lesson: We must respect the nature of those we love and give them the freedom to be true to their purpose in life. She did this effortlessly with me, and I was beginning to understand why I needed to let Tom be Tom. Some of us are simply born to roam. Absorbing this wisdom was a tall order for a six-year-old, but then, I was no ordinary first-grader, as I kept reminding the people around me.

Anyway, that's the way I remember it.

––––––––––––––––

Jean Dohanyos is an attorney referee in the Juvenile Division of Oakland County, Michigan. She lives with her family in Royal Oak, Michigan.

Cats, no less liquid than their shadows, offer no angles to the wind. They slip, diminished, neat, through loopholes less than themselves.

—A. S. J. Tessimond

My Vineyard Cats

Jan Steiger

We own a vineyard and know firsthand the amount of time and care it takes to grow grapes that produce excellent wines. It's enough work doing that without having to worry about rodents and other small animals that eat the grapes and destroy the plants as well. That's why we have our five kitties: Lacey, Blue, Little Girl, Red, and Jesse.

All of our cats are great hunters and like to bring their victims to the front door. They'll sit there with a gnarled rodent of some sort at their feet and let out a very strange cry, as if to say, "Hey, come look at what I caught!" They're all proud of what they catch—they're show-offs. I praise them for catching gophers, moles, mice, and other small animals, but try to discourage them from catching birds. If they do bring a bird, I try to save it before it is eaten.

Oddly, rabbits are the biggest problem we have, and the cats stay away from them because the rabbits are as big as the cats are! The same goes for possums and skunks. We also have a raccoon who comes up on the porch and helps itself to whatever cat food is left in their bowl. The cats just sit there and watch.

Lacey is a white longhaired male and my favorite of the cats. He likes to cuddle in my arms. I've owned plenty of cats but he's the only one I've ever seen who likes to suck his thumb! I've seen cats suck on cloth, hair, and other strange things, but Lacey prefers to cuddle up and suck on his thumb just like a baby. It's both annoying and cute. At times he seems to be the dominant one of the group.

Rather than use five separate bowls, I feed the cats in one big dish. Lacey will wait patiently for his turn, then he will reach out with one of his big paws and pull the bowl over to where he is sitting and enjoy a meal. None of the other cats bothers him.

The cats will follow me around the yard and driveway, but rarely will they follow me to into the vineyard—probably afraid of running into a wild rabbit!

Jan Steiger and her husband live near their vineyard in St. Helena, California, with their five cats. They are currently building a winery. Jan belongs to We Care, an organization dedicated to saving stray cats and dogs as well as cats and dogs whose owners have died or who can no longer care for themselves. Jan is the daughter of the famous singer Frankie Lane.

The only mystery about the cat is why it ever decided to become a domestic animal.

—Sir Compton MacKenzie

Cat Scratch Fever?

Ronnie Schell

Here is my one and only cat story. It's a true story and I have been telling it for years at social gatherings and on TV talk shows. I have owned only one cat in my entire life and her name was Kim. I actually inherited part ownership of Kim, a beautiful Persian, when I married my wife, Jan. She had owned Kim for about a year before we got together, so of course, when we got our first apartment as newlyweds, Kim came with us.

Ronnie Schell

Anyway, about a week after our honeymoon, we were settling in to our new domestic ways and one night, as newlyweds often do, we decided to engage in some amorous fun. Since it was very warm that evening, we were lying on top of the covers of our bed.

Everything was proceeding along fine when all of a sudden, from out of nowhere, our cat Kim made a giant leap onto the bed and immediately pounced on me just below my midsection! Thankfully, I leaped off the bed and fell to the floor before Kim's claws could do any real harm. Meanwhile Jan rolled over in hysterical laughter.

Needless to say, Kim was never allowed to spend any time in our bedroom again. To this day I don't know why she attacked me when and where she did, but after this nearly harrowing event, I became very close to Kim; when she passed away at the age of eighteen, I felt extremely sad. And although we got off to a rocky start, little Kim turned this dogs-only person into a real cat lover.

Ronnie Schell is an actor, director, writer, and comedian. For seven years he played Duke Slater, Gomer Pyle's sidekick on *Gomer Pyle* and *The Jim Nabors Hour.*

If a dog jumps in your lap, it's because he is fond of you;
but if a cat does the same thing, it is because your lap is warmer.

—Alfred North Whitehead

Don't Judge a Cat by His Chambers

Judge David Breck

In my many years in the legal profession, as an attorney, city mayor, and circuit court judge, I've witnessed more than my share of intense arguments (mostly between combative attorneys) that epitomize the phrase *natural-born enemy*. I've tried everything to keep a calm office but only recently discovered the most powerful nonprescription "attorney sedative" ever known to exist—a cat!

It happened quite by accident, actually. A beautiful Himalayan cat of mine had recently passed away and I wanted a new one to fill the void. I walked into the Humane Society, and for some unknown reason one cat in particular caught my eye. He was a beautiful longhaired mix who was scheduled to be euthanized. I couldn't resist. I named him Spooky and took him home.

I decided one day to take him to court with me, figuring he could stay in my chambers while I was on the bench. I had a meeting scheduled in my chambers later that day with two opposing attorneys. They became agitated and began to argue. About that same time Spooky appeared out of nowhere, I suppose to see what all the fuss was. It startled the attorneys a bit at first, but I saw a dramatic difference in the attitudes of both attorneys and the whole tenor of the discussion after Spooky appeared. I knew then I had discovered something very useful. He's a great facilitator and he works for kibble! What more could I want?

Spooky became a fixture and now basically has the run of the office.

Judge David Breck with Spooky, the peacekeeper, in his chambers
Photo by Melissa Wawzysko

Like most cats, he has a mischievous side. When no one is looking he'll crawl up on the coffee table and drink from the container we keep for making fresh coffee. He also has a habit of stepping on computer keys while people are away from their desks. It's not uncommon to come back to your desk and see all your settings changed.

Spooky and I are alike in many ways. We both like women, we both like to sleep, we enjoy lawyers, and we like having our stomachs rubbed. Of course, one major difference is that I have a law degree and he doesn't even have a pedigree. Still, it's a good match. I'm truly convinced that if more judges kept cats in their chambers, there might be a lot less for us to do.

The Honorable David Breck is an attorney, former mayor
of Birmingham, Michigan, and current circuit judge in
Oakland County, Michigan.

Of Manners and Irony

Elizabeth Perkin

I have loved cats for as long as I can remember. When I was younger, we had a cat named Dusty. Dusty was actually my mom's cat—a beautiful, gray, sleek little cat with exquisite manners. She was every inch a lady and no one was ever allowed to forget it. Everything she did, she did with grace and style. She ate in little bites, sat just so in chairs, and conducted herself with an air of total propriety.

One evening the air was filled with the screaming of stray cats. We looked outside and there in the middle of the street were two big tomcats fighting pretty fiercely. My mom opened the door to go out and shoo them away, and when she did, Dusty scooted past her. To our dismay, we watched Dusty trot right up to the tomcats. She raised one delicate little paw, and *Whap* smacked one of the cats right across the face! After all, this was Dusty, and the decorum must be kept.

My mom and I were ready to spring into action, certain that Dusty was now about to be killed. The tomcats just stared at her in amazement and suddenly bolted off. Dusty calmly turned around and came back into the house. I could have sworn that when she passed me I could hear her mutter, "Hoodlums!"

I took my love of cats with me when I moved out on my own, having as many as four at one time. I recently acquired a new kitten, who, like so many of my cats, was a little homeless boy who managed (without much difficulty) to thrust his way into my heart and home. Jesse wasn't very big when I brought him in, but little did I realize he was three pounds of hell-cat: loving, fun, unadulterated hell!

I already had two cats, Emily and Esmerelda, older girls who were quite set in their ways, and Jesse felt it was his moral obligation to terrorize them at any and every given opportunity.

Granted, it's pretty funny to watch a little three-pound kitten chase after a howling twelve-pound cat, but I'm sure the twelve-pound cat would disagree.

In addition to two adult cats and a kitten, my husband, Alan, and I also own ferrets, whom Jesse learned quite quickly weren't nearly as readily frightened as the older cats. His paw only had to land in their mouths a few times before he realized he was truly better off staying out of their room. After Alan built the ferrets a roomy cage, it didn't take long for Jesse to realize that he could torment the animals simply by running around in front of them, causing them no end of agitation.

Well, one Saturday afternoon, we came home from work and entered our house to hear some pretty pitiful meowing. Upon hastened investigation, we found Jesse in the room with the caged ferrets, only this time he himself was imprisoned! Apparently, as he'd been bouncing around impressing them with his freedom, he'd knocked over a cat carrier that was balanced on a chair. The opening of the carrier landed right over Jesse and jammed shut, leaving him stuck, much to the ferrets' delight (not to mention ours)!

———————————

Elizabeth Perkin is a test administrator at Wayne State University and lives comfortably with Alan, her three cats, two well-behaved ferrets, and a new dog.

There are many intelligent species in the universe. They are owned by cats.

—Anonymous

Half the Tongue—Twice the Volume

Pat Zuriech

My twenty-year-old male Siamese cat, Zimm, is one of the nicest, most affectionate cats I've ever met, and perhaps one of the strangest ones, too. I'd heard stories about the kind of temperament Siamese cats possess, but now I believe them.

I first got Zimm as an eight-month-old kitten from a family that was moving to an apartment in Boston that didn't allow animals. I gave him the name Zimm, which was my nickname when I'd played minor-league baseball for the Detroit Tigers. He's an indoor cat but occasionally we let him out to eat grass and whatever else he finds.

Zimm's strangeness isn't made up of any one certain thing; instead, it's a collection of little oddities that make up who he is. First of all, he's the loudest cat I've ever heard. He doesn't merely meow, he screams—all the time! Years ago we lived in an apartment, and we used to get a lot of complaints from the neighbors about his noisemaking. You could hear him three or four doors down. Even now, in our house, dinner guests and especially overnight guests remark that he is one loud creature.

At only seven pounds, you wouldn't think he could muster up the lung capacity to project so much guttural volume, but he does, and after a while it can drive people nuts. Picture the Scarecrow with Pavarotti's loudness, and you've described Zimm. And he does this even though he has only half of his tongue. That's how he was when we got him. Most of the time his noise doesn't bother us. I guess we've simply gotten used to it.

Zimm sleeps during the day, storing up energy, I'm sure, then wakes up when we come home. He basically screams all evening and night. He's constantly following one of us around, no matter where we go in the house. He loves attention and likes to get patted. Not the soft, gentle kind of patting, but firm patting, like a dog would want.

We thought if we got him a kitten as a playmate he would stay up during the day hours and sleep at night. Instead, he went on a hunger strike, refusing to eat or drink anything for days. On the advice of our vet we gave the kitten away. Within days, Zimm was back to his normal self.

Most cats have favorite dishes they like to eat or drink from. Not Zimm. He will only drink from potted plants that have just been watered. Needless to say, the plants in our house are always watered. His favorite plant to drink from used to be located on an old piano. He would jump up for a quick drink, then serenade us by walking up and down the keyboard. Anything to make more noise!

Oddly enough, with all the noise Zimm likes to make, he's petrified of the noise our vacuum cleaner makes. He spends a lot of time in our bedroom and whenever we want him out, we simply turn on the vacuum cleaner. We keep the vacuum there for just such an occasion. Despite his eccentricities, it's been a real pleasure to have him.

Pat Zuriech owns a residential and commercial painting company,
Pat's Fine Line Painting, and lives with his family
in Westland, Michigan.

Ignorant people think it is the noise which fighting cats
make that is so aggravating, but it ain't so;
it is the sickening grammar that they use.

—Mark Twain

Cats, Their Owners, and Anecdotes

Jim Humphries, D.V.M.

One of the more interesting questions I am sometimes asked is, What is the difference between cats and dogs, their owners, and the bonding process between each? My response? Personality—the animal's and the owner's.

People who own cats tend to be more independent than other people and seem to like the soft side of things. They are enamored by the aloof, know-it-all, curious nature of cats. They are also intrigued by the cat's ability to get in trouble and make it look purposeful, or to do really stupid, aggressive things like dart across the room and look over as if to say, "Gee, who did that?" Cats are fastidious.

Dog owners are typically miffed by these qualities. Unlike cats, dogs desperately need people. If not for people, dogs would be in trouble all the time, getting injured or killed. They tend to be gregarious and nonindependent thinkers. They work best with discipline and a leash. Cats are just the opposite.

The human-animal bond differs, too: When you bond with a feline, you've earned it, according to the cat's standards, and nobody but the cat knows what those standards are. When you bond with a dog, though, it's because you've bought it with time, treats, food, and attention. Despite these differences, both animals play an important role in our lives.

I currently have three cats, Indi, Little Bit, and BC—all rescued cats who have provided me with a lot of entertaining moments over the years.

My wife and I were living in Dallas when we found Indi. We were out one night walking our trained German shepherd after a hard rain when I heard an itty-bitty, pitiful meow. I looked down and in the dimly lit street saw a tiny gray ball of lint about to be washed down the storm drain. I approached the kitten very carefully, so as not to scare him into running into the drain.

I called to the kitten and he bounded over to me and leaped into my lap, all wet and shaky, and clung to me with his claws. I said, "That's it, you got a home now, buddy." We named him Indi after the movie character Indiana Jones. I was amazed at how the kitten recognized that help was there. Many cats in that kind of trouble get so frightened they run the other way. I did make one mistake with him, however. When I took him home and began drying him off, I decided it was time for him to meet Zeus, our German shepherd. That cat let out a loud hiss, clawed me, and took off. About fifteen minutes later, crawling under two cars, I got him back. It's probably not the best way to introduce dogs and cats!

We recently moved from Dallas to a forty-acre horse farm about twenty-five miles north of Colorado Springs. The property included a run-down barn that had a cat as its sole resident. We decided to keep him and named him BC, for Barn Cat. He's a big, friendly cat who loves attention and is great at catching mice.

Just a few weeks after we moved here we had the blizzard of the century, with three straight days of seventy-mile-per-hour wind and over ninety-six inches of snow, which easily reached up to the second-story windows of the house. The windchill was well below zero. The old-timers said they had never seen anything as bad as this. It was blowing so much that I couldn't even imagine what it looked like in the barn, where snow tends to drift in through the littlest of cracks.

About two days into the blizzard we realized we had to go down to the barn and take care of BC—if we could get there. My wife and I concocted a plan to take a heated pet bed—made from a small fiberglass travel kennel, three blankets, a heating pad, and an extension cord—to the cat. It meant I would have to walk four hundred feet in over six feet of freezing snow to make this cat a warm bed.

The weather was so bad I couldn't see ten feet in front of me. Plus the area was so new to us that I didn't have my bearings straight yet. The minute I took a step, my tracks were covered up. It was risky, but nonetheless the cat had to have a warm bed.

I finally made it to the barn only to discover the entire barn floor was covered in snow. BC was up in the rafters. I got a rickety ladder and teetered on the top step on my tiptoes, trying to rig a heated cat bed inside a travel kennel with blankets underneath and on top, and an electric blanket inside. The electric cord had to be strung down a certain way to keep it safe for the cat. (Thankfully, the storm hadn't knocked out the barn's power.) All this so the cat could have a warm place to sleep. Ever since then he's been my special friend.

Jim Humphries is a media veterinarian, serving as a product-development consultant for the industry and a spokesperson for various companies. He owns a video production company that produces animal training films, cable shows, and commercials. His show *Great Pets* is seen on 150 stations throughout the United States. Jim is also the author of *Dr. Jim's Animal Clinic for Cats*. He and his wife live near Colorado Springs, Colorado.

Cats possess so many of the same qualities as some people that it is often hard to tell the people and the cats apart.

—P. J. O'Rourke

Communicating With Your Pets

Sonya Fitzpatrick

When I was a child, we lived in a rural area of Britain, and I can recall getting in all sorts of trouble with my parents because I knew all the village gossip. They thought I was eavesdropping on people, when in fact it was the animals who were telling me things about their owners. I had a special gift—I could communicate with animals.

Animals are intelligent, spiritual beings. They can sense how we feel about them, because we're always sending out telepathic images subconsciously. (This happens in people as well, through the electromagnetic fields of our bodies.) I use this gift to bring about healing in all sorts of animals. While there is a lot of satisfaction in healing and treating animals, one of the biggest joys of having this gift is being able to reunite owners with their lost pets.

We have many animals in our home, some we've purchased and some we've adopted. The oldest member of our animal family is an eighteen-year-old cat named Wellington, whom we brought to the United States from England.

Cats are very intelligent, very sensitive animals. They are the most independent of all household pets. Some are very affectionate and will follow you around, while others want no physical contact at all. They are as different in personality as humans are. Think about all the personali-

Sonya Fitzpatrick and her beloved eighteen-year-old cat, Wellington

ties you meet in everyday life; some people are extroverts, while other are completely introverted. This is true with cats, too.

Many people like cats because they are low maintenance—easy to care for, especially when they're declawed. People who declaw their cat for the sake of saving their furniture don't understand that it's a form of mutilation and makes a cat feel sad and useless. In many European countries declawing a cat is against the law, and understandably so.

If you truly love your cat, declawing it is the cruelest thing you can do. Imagine what it's like having the ends of your fingers removed. Cats are very trainable and a good scratching post is the answer.

The following story of Pebbles the cat is but one example of how I am able to help animals.

I was called by my client, Luan, a lovely Chinese lady whose pets I had worked with many times. She was upset because Pebbles, one of her three cats, had suddenly forced Timmy, another of her cats, into a corner and wouldn't let him come out. Every time poor Timmy tried to leave the corner, Pebbles would attack him, biting and scratching, until Timmy had no choice but to retreat.

The one time Luan tried to intervene, Pebbles had bitten her, too—a fact that amazed her, because in their seven years together the cat had never been anything other than a loving and gentle companion.

I connected to Pebbles telepathically. He was very angry. I asked Pebbles, "Why are you attacking Timmy?"

Pebbles responded quite simply, "Timmy has a strange scent. If he moves out of the corner he will make everything smell strange."

I now understood why I'd been having an uncomfortable feeling in my nose, but I still didn't know why Pebbles had bitten Luan. "Why did you bite Luan, Pebbles? You have never bitten before."

"If she had picked Timmy up, she would have smelled like him, so I bit her to keep her from picking him up," Pebbles said.

Seen from the point of view of the animal, it was all so logical. I asked Luan if she had put a new spray or powder on Timmy and she told me she'd bought a new homeopathic flea remedy because Timmy had a terrible infestation of fleas, and she was afraid to use a poison on him. I wondered when she had employed the new treatment. "A few days ago," she told me. Then I asked her if this was when Pebbles had changed his behavior toward Timmy, and she answered that it was. Pebbles, compared to most cats, has a heightened sense of smell. I reminded Luan of a previous incident when Pebbles had reacted to the scent of a new perfume she had started wearing by refusing to come near her. Apparently, the odor of the flea remedy was also offensive to his sensitive nose.

Sonya Fitzpatrick realized at a very early age that she had the innate ability to communicate with animals. She does this not through words, but by connecting telepathically with an animal to receive emotions, feelings, and pictures, which she puts into words. Some call her a modern-day Dr. Doolittle. She treats physical and psychological pet problems and provides instruction for pet owners to help them communicate with their pets.

Sonya is author of the popular book *What the Animals Tell Me* and a former top international model. Originally from Britain, she currently lives and practices in Houston, Texas.

Women, poets, and especially artists, like cats; delicate natures only can realize their sensitive systems.

—Helen M. Winslow,
American writer

Curiosity Almost Did Kill the Cat

Mike Myers

We have a ten-pound shorthair named Mr. Cat who is one of the most curious cats I have ever known. Mr. Cat likes to follow me around to see what's going on, I suppose thinking he might miss something important. Because we work out of a home office, we're used to seeing Mr. Cat quite a bit.

One morning I had an important meeting, so I went to the laundry room to wash a shirt and other things. As usual, Mr. Cat followed me to the room and sat up near the washer opening to watch everything I was doing. He liked to bat at the water that was filling the washing machine as I put the clothes in.

Once the clothes were done, I went to the laundry room to remove them from the dryer, which has a spring-loaded, front-facing door that pulls downward. I thought the dryer door had shut when I was finished, but apparently, it had not. Mr. Cat, to his detriment, was curious about what was inside and no doubt was attracted by the warmth. Unbeknownst to me, he leaped up on the lid and crawled inside. The weight of him leaping on the dryer door activated the spring and the door slammed shut behind him. Mr. Cat was the type of cat who roamed all over the house in search of mischief or a place to curl up, so I never realized he was gone.

It was quite late in the afternoon before I realized I hadn't seen him in a while. I did a quick tour of the house, but no cat. I figured he was

Mr. Cat, lord of the carpet

hiding someplace. A short time later I began to hear very strange noises that resembled an animal, but I couldn't determine where they were coming from. They finally led me to the dryer in the laundry room.

Nothing on earth could have prepared me for the smell that came out of that dryer when I opened the door! Mr. Cat had obviously panicked at some point, losing all control of bowel and bladder function.

I found him running in place, spinning the dryer drum around and around like a hamster wheel, with the feces flying all about. I immediately took the cat and myself to the shower and jumped in. It took a while for the smell and mess to come off him.

Once he was out of harm's way, I returned to the dryer to try to clean it out. About that time, my fiancée, Anne, came home from her meeting to find me cleaning out the dryer with a white sock tied around my head to keep from breathing the smell! What a sight that must have been. She was an angel about the whole thing. She helped me clean it out, although it took a good long time. Ever since then, Mr. Cat will occasionally follow me into the laundry room, but he won't even go near the washer or dryer.

Mike Myers is co-owner of an Internet service provider and Web site design firm in Frederick, Maryland.

Home Invasion of a Cat Kind

Susan Jackson

W e live in a usually quiet neighborhood in the Detroit suburbs with our three cats. At one time we had six, but a few eventually passed on. Our cats are all indoor cats, and to amuse them we built a special outdoor "kitty condo" where they can exercise. It's a fifteen-by twenty-foot, six-foot-high, fully enclosed area that is accessible through a cat door leading from a bedroom window. An attached ramp lets the cats get to and from the window. The cats really enjoy being able to play "outdoors."

Stray cats must somehow know that we're cat people because twice in recent years our home has been invaded by a stray cat. The first visit came when we lived in a town house. We were taking care of three cats for my boyfriend's sister, which meant we had six cats in the house. They all seemed to get along, provided "personal space" was respected. One of the sister's cats—a beautiful gray cat who limped—was named Piggy. After we'd had the cats for a while, we started noticing that the food we put out was instantly gone, every day. We then came home from work one afternoon and noticed that one of the cats had urinated on the kitchen counter. This seemed strange to both of us, because none of the cats had ever done this before. This went on for about two weeks.

Well, one Friday evening we came home and Steven went upstairs to change, while I fed the cats in the kitchen. He called down to me, asking me to call Piggy down for dinner. I replied that I didn't have to, because

Piggy was with me in the kitchen. He said, "No she's not, she's up here in the hallway." I said, "You're nuts. Piggy is sitting right here in the kitchen." He came to the kitchen and saw Piggy sitting beside me. "Something is really bizarre here," he said, "because Piggy is up in the hall."

We went upstairs, got the other cat, and brought him down. They were identical twins. It was uncanny! The only way we could tell them apart was that Piggy limped and this one didn't. What we didn't know was that one of our basement windows was broken; the other cat had crawled in and been living with us for two weeks. We took him to the Humane Society.

The most recent incident happened at our new home with the attached kitty condo. For about three weeks before the latest invasion I noticed a stray black cat hanging around the outdoor enclosure. He liked to climb up the fencing, lie on top, and tease the other cats by hissing and yowling. We would chase him away by spraying him with water or banging on the window. It was pretty aggravating.

One day while we were at work, the black cat apparently fell through the chicken-wire cover and landed inside the enclosure. He probably chased our cats around the condo, then followed them into the bedroom through the cat door in the window. When we came home, we heard the blinds rattling in the bedroom. I walked in there and started to yell at Edsel, my black-and-white cat, only to notice that Edsel was sitting behind me. That's when I knew we had another intruder. I put Edsel in another room, went back inside the bedroom, closed the door, and hoped to catch the black cat.

I realized I had a big problem. I tried talking to the cat, but he was in an absolute panic. He had a wild, glazed look in his eyes and wanted no part of my comforting words. I called out to Steven for help, knowing I wasn't going to catch this cat alone. This crazy cat was trying to get to someplace high, so he was airborne—leaping from place to place. He jumped at the window, thinking he could get out, but all he succeeded in doing was catching himself in the mini blinds, dangling and struggling to get free.

We tried to cover him with towels, not knowing if he had claws, but he panicked even more. He wriggled free and began leaping about, knocking things over. First it was the computer monitor, keyboard, and speakers, then it was the hanging plant. Dirt was showering everywhere and, of course, the cat was urinating freely wherever he landed. It was a mess!

After the better part of forty-five minutes the cat finally tired out, at least somewhat, and we were able to wrap him in towels and put him into one of our cat carriers. We couldn't get the towels off from around him to close the carrier completely, so we fastened one side, used a bungee cord to hold the other, and used duct tape and cardboard to close the front. It looked like we had some sort of grotesque creature from another planet inside. I'll never forget the looks we got when we arrived at the police station. One officer cautiously peeked around the corner at the carrier held together with bungees and duct tape, still wiggling from the cat trying to free himself, and asked, "Um . . . what do you have in there?" I said, "Don't worry—it's only a crazed cat!"

The cat was taken to the police animal pound and eventually to the Humane Society. Once he calmed down, he was actually a beautiful, affectionate cat. As for our kitty condo, the roof is now repaired, and no other break-ins have been reported—although we are on constant alert!

———————

Susan Jackson is a health educator who lives with her boyfriend,
Steven, and their three cats.

A baited cat may grow as fierce as a lion.

—Samuel Palmer

Electrified Kitties

Roberta Dunn

In the mid-1970s our family was offered a Siamese kitten. We had heard stories about how mean Siamese cats can be, but this one was simply too adorable to refuse. Both my sister and I became very attached to our new kitty. In 1981, my sister went away to nursing school; upon completion, she decided to get married. I had the cat all to myself.

Once my sister and her new husband were all settled in to their new home, she decided she could no longer stand not having a cat. Her husband surprised her by buying a Siamese kitten. She was thrilled! They both worked full time, so within six months they'd decided to buy a new kitten to keep the first one company. The cats loved to sleep on the bed, especially in the winter, because my sister had an electric blanket. The cats were in heaven!

After five years of marriage, my sister and brother-in-law decided it was time to start a family. Knowing that cats aren't always fond of newborns, they asked me if I would adopt theirs. I was thrilled! I'm not really fond of cats sleeping on the bed, so I quickly learned that the only way to keep them off was to buy them their own electric blanket and make a little bed for them. It's truly a sight to see the cats sleeping comfortably in their own mini bed with their own electric blanket that's on twenty-four hours a day, all year round!

Roberta Dunn works as a family court clerk and lives
with her two kitties.

Cat Fact Quiz 4

Myths

TRUE OR FALSE
1. Catgut, routinely used to make violin strings and tennis racquets, actually comes from cats.
2. Cats can be taught to walk on a leash.
3. Cats can learn many kinds of tricks.
4. Cats are extremely good learners.
5. Cats always land on their feet when they fall.

ANSWERS
1. *False.* Catgut, doesn't come from cats. It actually comes from sheep, hogs, and horses.
2. *True.* Although many owners will disagree, cats can be taught to walk on a leash. Some cats do quite well at it.
3. *True.* Like dogs, cats can be taught many tasks and tricks, including using a toilet as well as sitting, begging, playing dead, and more.
4. *True.* Cats have exceptional memories and exhibit a significant knack for learning through experience and observing their environments.
5. *False.* It depends on the distance from which the cat falls. The higher the distance, the more likely it is to land on its feet.

Losing My Best Buddy

DeAnna Heil

My husband and I bought our first house almost three years ago. Soon after we moved in, a small calico cat appeared in our doorway, hungry and lonely. We fed her once, and, of course, she never went away. We named her Mamma and decided to adopt her as our own. She had several batches of kittens before we had her spayed. We found good homes for all but four, whom we ended up keeping over the years. Tango and Cash were from her first litter. Tango was a calico female, Cash an orange male. They grew up together playing and fighting. They were just like any human brother and sister would be.

Tango was the independent, outgoing one. Cash was the loving cat who never wanted us to put him down. He was the first one at the door to greet us, and the one to follow us around the house weaving in and out of our feet. He was vocal and let us know what he was thinking. He was lazy, really lazy. It's said that most cats sleep twelve to sixteen hours a day. Well, I think Cash slept twenty-two!

One night we noticed that Cash was acting rather peculiar. He would look up at us and meow, but we couldn't tell that anything was really wrong. He just seemed to be in pain. We decided to wait until the next morning to see if he acted differently. The next morning came and Cash still wasn't any better. In fact, he seemed worse. He wouldn't walk and he was really jittery. I called the vet, who told me to bring him in right away.

The vet examined him and said that overnight, some crystals had built up in Cash's urethra that stopped him from being able to urinate; in turn, this had poisoned him from the inside. He had feline urinary syndrome. I was devastated. We ended up having him put down.

Today Tango, Mamma, and Ms. Sweets keep me company. Tango has taken over some of the qualities of her late brother. She is much more affectionate now and loves to lie in my lap. She is also very vocal, but she still doesn't replace the friend I lost. My three calico cats offer me wonderful company and entertainment.

DeAnna Heil is currently a student. She and her husband live
in Twin Falls, Idaho.

One of the ways in which cats show happiness is by sleeping.

—Cleveland Amory

Madcap Kitty and Other Remembrances

Ernie Harwell

We've owned a lot of cats over the years. Being a sports broadcaster meant that I was on the road a lot, and cats always seemed nice to come home to—they have sort of a calming, relaxing effect. At one time, in our Florida home, we owned four or five cats who basically lived in our garage. We left the garage door open and had a neighborhood boy feed them for us. Sadly, we lost one to a rattlesnake. We took him to the vet for treatment, but it was too late.

Another cat we had, in our Michigan home, was named Velvet. She was a good cat, but not always as soft spoken as her name would imply. One day my wife, Lula, noticed Velvet was sleeping on the edge of our bed, which we don't particularly care for. When Lula tried to move Velvet off the bed, she startled the cat, and Lula got bitten and had to go to the hospital for stitches and a tetanus shot.

We currently have one of the craziest cats we've ever owned. She's always making us laugh by getting into some sort of trouble, mostly harmless. She's a one-year-old calico named Patches, aptly named for the many different-colored patches in her fur. We've kind of inherited her on a part-time basis from our daughter Julie. When Patches was declawed and spayed, Julie asked us to baby-sit. Patches took to our place right away and has since become part of the family.

We've given her a few nicknames for the messes she seems to get herself into. For a while we called her Chimney Sweep. It seems one day she decided to investigate the fireplace and ended up climbing partly up the chimney. She was covered in soot and had to be taken to the vet for a good scrubbing. Not too long after that she did it again, which required another trip to the vet. Finally she realized that climbing up the chimney meant going to the vet, not one of her favorite things, and she's never done it again.

We also called her Kramer for a while because she reminded us of Michael Richards's character from *Seinfeld.* One minute she was in one spot, the next minute she was zooming to another, seemingly without purpose. She would come racing into a room and crash into furniture and things or slide on the floor. She's crazy like Kramer!

We recently purchased a videotape for her that has birds, butterflies, and fish. She sits very attentively watching the action and often tries to claw or eat her way through the TV screen. She's one nutty cat, to be sure.

Ernie Harwell with crazy cat, Patches
Photo by Melissa Wawzysko

Ernie Harwell is a Baseball Hall of Fame radio and TV announcer with over fifty years in the big leagues, the last thirty-nine with the Detroit Tigers and CBS Radio. He and his wife, Lula, divide their time between Florida and Michigan.

The trouble with a kitten is that / It eventually becomes a cat.

—Ogden Nash

The Kilkenny Cats

Traditional

There wanst was two cats in Kilkenny,
Each thought there was one cat too many,
    So they quarrel'd and fit, they scratched and they bit,
    'Til excepting their nails, and the tips of their tails,
Instead of two cats, there wasn't any!

Sparky the Island Cat

Stacey Rogers

My husband, Ken (then a fiancé), and I found Sparky on an island on the Tennessee River, in Marion County. Ken's dad has a house on the river, which always seemed to have about fifteen or so cats hanging around. They were all feral (wild) cats and wouldn't let anyone get very close to them. One cat in particular, however, was very friendly and constantly meowed to be petted and scratched. He was definitely different from the rest. He was about six months old when he appeared. That was Sparky.

After Ken and I got married we realized we wanted to have a cat. I had always had cats growing up. We decided to bring Sparky home, since he was somewhat attached to us already. We took a cat carrier to Ken's dad's house to get Sparky. We were able to get him safely in the carrier, but the rest of the way back wasn't as easy. To get to and from the island we used a motorboat. Sparky hated the noise and hated the ride and howled loudly, as if he were being maimed, for the whole trip.

This continued once he was in the car as well. He was frantic, and by the time we got home, he had begun to drool. I thought we had traumatized him for life, but he got over it. Still, even now he hates car rides to the vet! The only way we can get him to settle down in the car is to play "Nada Nos Separara" by Jose Feliciano.

Sparky is a friendly cat, but at one time he didn't like to be held for very long. Anyone's lap is the last place you would find him. However, Sparky survived two natural disasters that turned him from an indepen-

Sparky with a collection of Christmas goodies

dent to a big baby. First, we had a record-breaking blizzard in 1993, and then a tornado hit our house in March 1997. The second one was scarier for Sparky, especially since he used to sleep in the garage. He was so terrified he actually crawled up on my lap. Now it's hard for me to get him out of my lap, and he even sleeps in the bedroom with us sometimes.

Sparky has some habits that are very funny to watch. He's an indoor-outdoor cat and we don't keep a litter box in the house for him. When he's done outside, he jumps up on the porch swing, meows very loudly, and swings back and forth until we let him in. It's hilarious to see. He also likes to tease the neighbor's Labrador retriever by prancing in front of the fence and meowing. Some of our funny nicknames for Sparky are Pookie Bear, Shnookems, the King of Pook, Lord Retard, and Lord Sparkton.

Stacey Rogers lives in Chattanooga, Tennessee, with her husband, Ken, and their cat, Sparky. She works as secretary to the director of Information Services at McKee Corporation, maker of Little Debbie's Snacks.

Fastest Mouser in the East Gets Jury Duty Call

Lia Graceffa

I'll never forget the blizzard of 1978, when the entire Boston area was buried under a thick blanket of snow. The snow made it impossible for mice to find food, so they all came indoors, creating a problem for people throughout the city. Many people bought cats to keep their house free of mice and the little surprises they leave behind. In 1980, having exhausted every other means of keeping my own house mouse-free, I got a kitten. I was traveling through Maine when I got her and decided to name her Cat Mousam, after the road we were traveling on. We called her Mouser for short, and she certainly lived up to her name. Soon after that, we got Mouser a playmate, Leo.

Mouser was very beautiful, but one of the most unfriendly cats I had ever come across. It was rare that I could pet or scratch her, and friends didn't dare go near her for fear of being clawed. She was excellent at catching mice, though, so I pretty much let her have her freedom. She was like this for a little over ten years.

Now, over the years I've received some interesting mail—not to mention the usual assortment of junk mail—but in July 1985 an official-looking letter arrived that threw me a bit. It was addressed to Cat Mousam. I thought it was a joke at first, but upon further inspection I learned it was from the county offices. Cat Mousam had been summoned for jury duty later that summer! I couldn't believe it.

There was a form enclosed that permitted prospective jurors to offer reasons why they couldn't serve. I explained on the form that Mousam couldn't speak the language and was, in fact, a cat. A few weeks later Cat Mousam received an official letter from the Massachusetts jury commissioner excusing her from service. The official reason given for the pardon was: "Language."

I found out later from the jury commissioner's office that because Cat Mousam's name appears on the front door of my home, the census taker assumed Cat Mousam was a person. I was assured that the system was going to be fixed and this wouldn't happen again. Imagine my surprise when, eight months later, Leo received the same type of summons for jury duty. So much for our census system.

It's interesting how different Mousam and Leo were for the first ten years. Leo was the cuddly cat, while Mousam was happy being alone. Something changed in Mousam, though, and she seemed to mellow in the last five or six years of her life. She actually became quite affectionate toward the end. She died at home on October 8, 1996, at sixteen years of age. I knew she had been sick for a while and was probably holding on just for me. I held her in my lap for about a half hour one day before work. I gently stroked her and told her it was all right to go. She died later that day.

Lia Graceffa lives and works as a social worker near Boston, Massachusetts. She currently has a dog named Evita and a cat named Miss Kitty.

A dog is a dog, a bird is a bird, a cat is a person.

—Mugsy Peabody

Using the Power of Touch to Help Your Cat

Amy D. Shojai

Numerous studies have been conducted over the years documenting the "pet effect"—people who keep pets live healthier, happier, and longer lives. Even people who are very sick or in nursing homes tend to improve when they have contact with a pet. But what's really neat is that the pet effect works both ways: Touching your cat boosts her health, too.

Massage and acupressure help a wide range of health conditions, and both techniques have gained acceptance by veterinarians around the country. In fact, in 1996 the American Veterinary Medicine Association (AVMA) approved acupuncture and its cousin acupressure, calling them an "integral part of veterinary medicine." And an added benefit is that hands-on treatments such as massage and acupressure can be safely and effectively performed by owners at home.

Massage therapy is used to treat the soft tissues in the body, specifically the muscles and tendons. Massage helps keep Kitty limber, so she can move more easily. This is especially helpful for older arthritic cats who tend to stiffen up; when it hurts to move, their grooming tends to suffer. When it's no longer easy to stick that leg up overhead anymore, a cat tends to lose the spit-and-polish. And as all cat lovers know, a clean cat is a happy cat, and dinginess makes the cat feel even worse. After a nice session of massage that warms up the muscles, though, even an arthritic cat typically stretches and finishes with a head-to-toe grooming session.

Like most touch therapies, massage is also a great stress relief. Stress is related to a variety of cat illnesses, including feline asthma. And because reducing stress can boost the immune system, a massage helps Kitty stay healthier and recover more quickly if she does become ill or needs surgery.

The easiest technique is to simply begin at your cat's head, and use even, rhythmic strokes with your palm down the length of her body. The cat will tell you to press harder by arching her back, or to lighten up by shrinking away; purring is a great indicator you've hit the target. And just think—you're relieving your own stress and deepening the bond with your cat at the very same time.

Acupressure is based on the Chinese traditional medicine technique of acupuncture, but instead of needles (which only a certified veterinary acupuncturist should use), acupressure uses the tips of the fingers—you simply press down firmly on the designated point for ten to fifteen seconds, then release. To be honest, nobody is sure exactly how this works, but acupressure can relieve problems from diarrhea to skin disease, pain, and even epilepsy. This technique stimulates certain places on the body that are focal points of nerve endings, which sends the healing message to sometimes distant places on the body. For example, pressing a point known as the "aspirin point" on a cat's ankle will relieve pain throughout her body—why, we aren't sure. There are hundreds of points on the cat's body, just like on other animals and people, and you should check with a vet familiar with the technique to show you which points will work best for your cat's particular ailment.

These healing therapies sound a bit like hocus-pocus to many people, but in fact, it doesn't really matter what you call them or how they work, as long as they help your cat. After all, every time you pet your cat, you're indulging in touch therapy, whether you know it or not. And generally speaking, cats know what they like and what they want. Many cats, once they've experienced the joys of massage, will become quite demanding and make themselves a nuisance until you rub them the right way. It's typical for arthritic pets to present you with the area of their body they want touched—a sore hip, for example, or the back of a stiff neck.

I recommend these therapies to many pet owners because they are a natural, safe, and effective way to help your cat at home. I even practice

Seren
Photo by Amy Shojai

them on my own cat, Serendipity, who loves the attention. Seren's a beautiful—and opinionated—champagne-mink Tonkinese cat with blue-jean-colored eyes. She was four months old when she was dumped on the back porch of a friend's house. (I have a real problem with people who think animals are a disposable commodity!) We're assuming she was the product of a backyard breeder and the last of a litter, who couldn't be placed in a home. The owner probably figured that dumping her in a good neighborhood would guarantee the kitten a good home. Seren was fortunate—other cats usually aren't nearly so lucky.

When my friend came home from a vacation, she immediately called me to say that there was a beautiful kitten sleeping in a big clay flowerpot on her back porch. I just happened to be catless at the time, and I wanted a cat, so I agreed to take a look. When I arrived, the kitten greeted me with a loud Siamese-like meow, jumped into my arms, gave me a whisker-kiss, then started purring. Seren decided I was the one and bull-dozed her way into my heart; I didn't have any choice.

My husband, though, wasn't so easily convinced. We had recently lost our thirteen-year-old German shepherd, and he wasn't ready to have another pet so soon. I reluctantly agreed to try to find Seren another home as soon as she was healthy again—she was very anemic and full of fleas—all the while hoping I wouldn't have to. I shouldn't have worried, because Seren knew what to do. She set out to melt his heart and did the job in three days flat. I knew she'd won and was here to stay when I came home and found the two of them sleeping on the couch, her body curled up on his stomach.

Seren is an energetic mischievous cat who likes to talk, climb, and get into everything, including my coffee mug in the morning. She's also my worst editor. There are teeth marks on every piece of paper in my office. She particularly likes the fax machine and printer, and waits to "ambush" the paper as it comes out. And she answers my phone when it rings (but refuses to hang it back up). After having missed many messages, I've learned to keep her out of my office when I'm not there.

Amy D. Shojai is the author of eleven books on pet health and behavior, and the president and founder of the Cat Writers' Association, an international group of professional cat writers. She lives with her husband and Serendipity in Sherman, Texas.

With the qualities of cleanliness, affection, patience, dignity, and courage that cats have, how many of us, I ask you, would be capable of becoming cats?

—Fernand Mery

Crabby Oskar, King of the Hill

Marcia Letzring

Oskar came to live with us in 1972 after I was divorced. The girls wanted a kitten and someone offered us Oskar. He was cute and cuddly, but little did we know that he would soon begin his life's task of training us in the way we were to go. From the beginning Oskar was a proud, regal animal who demanded and received homage. He grew into a large, powerful tomcat who had no equal.

One of the first things to change was the way toilet paper was handled. If we hung it on a roller, we would come home to find the paper strewn throughout the house. Oskar would apparently grab one end in his teeth and run down the hall, through the kitchen, into the dining room, through the living room, back down the hall into a bedroom, and continue until the roll ended. Of course, he always appeared innocent. We learned to place the toilet paper on the back of the toilet.

Facial tissue was the next to be changed. Pop-up tissue was his delight. He would sit on his hind legs and, alternating front paws, pull a tissue up, flinging it into the air—very rapidly. If caught, he would sit there looking at the tissue settling by his feet as if to say, "How did that get there?" We stopped buying pop-up tissue.

Oskar basically did not like people or animals. He accepted my children, though, and would permit them to treat him as a "baby" by dressing him in clothes and bonnets. My middle daughter had a parakeet, but the only place we could safely hang the cage was over the kitchen sink. Otherwise, we were apt to be awakened at two in the morning as the cat and bird had a confrontation.

Although the pet gerbils were kept in securely locked cages, I was greeted by my three-year-old son, Kurt, one day with, "Gerbil all gone." When I asked what had happened, he replied, "Kurt see gerbil. Kurt play with gerbil. Oskar see gerbil. All gone gerbil." We sadly retrieved the few bones left from behind the couch.

Oskar did enjoy and relate well to our border collie, Penny. She was a very determined, strong personality and was able to convince Oskar that she belonged to the house, also. In fact, they teamed up to keep the neighborhood free of unwanted dogs and cats, much to our neighbors' distress. Oskar methodically disposed of any male cat, even if he was someone's pet. Only female cats were allowed.

Other dogs we had as pets during Oskar's reign learned to submit to Oskar. They let him eat their food, share their beds, and, in general, have his way. When it came to people, Oskar had definite rules of conduct. He particularly disliked those who rushed up to him, picked him up, and tried to pet him. He would tolerate strangers, but only if they left him alone. He tended to disappear if unwanted attention was offered.

Oskar had ways of letting us know of his approval or disapproval of our actions. When we were good, we were rewarded with him sitting in our laps. When we had done something outstanding, we were given a freshly caught (thankfully dead) mouse. If he mildly disapproved, he would ignore us and not allow himself to be petted. When angry, he would leave a fecal deposit in the individual's shoe. Well, at least he did until I was late for work one day. My shoes were the last thing to go on. As I felt the "squish" and smelled the stink, my rage and reaction to Oskar were enough to convince him to change his ways. From then on he left his deposit on the person's pillow. It was more easily removed and washable!

Admittedly, I am not a great fan of cats, but Oskar and I respected each other. The test of our relationship came when Oskar returned after a three-day absence. He was coated in at least an inch of oily clay. He never could have gotten himself clean. After surveying the situation, with the cries of the children in the background, I developed a plan of action. Of course, I need not say that Oskar, like most cats, hated water. I resolutely picked him up, went in the bathroom, and locked the door behind us.

I filled the tub with warm, soapy water, tried to find Oskar (it's amazing how many places a cat can hide in a small bathroom), and finally put him in the tub, swishing him around until he yowled and scratched. At that point I let him go and he leaped out, snarling. He permitted me to grab him with a towel and rub him down. Slowly, the sticky, oily mess was removed. Four hours later we emerged from the bathroom. Oskar was almost clean, I was soaking wet and mildly scratched, and the bathroom was an absolute mess. Oskar could have severely injured me but seemed to know that I was helping him. I, in turn, wished he could have been more cooperative.

About this time, a friend of mine in graduate school happened to remark that she would soon turn forty-five years old and had never had a birthday party. I immediately organized a bash. On the night of the party, Oskar was well fed and willingly escaped outside to avoid meeting strange people. When my friend was opening her presents we heard Oskar yowling to come in. As I opened the door he dashed in, carrying the largest field rat I have ever seen, and laid it at her feet. That was one party no one will ever forget. What I don't understand is why *she* deserved a rat when we, the family, only rated mice!

When I completed graduate school and got a "real" job, we moved to a resort community. Oskar was delighted. We were in the "back" of the community, surrounded by woods. He hunted continuously. As usual, he refused to wear a collar, clawing off any we put on. This ultimately resulted in his death. A security guard decided to rid the area of all unclaimed pets and shot him, even though he knew Oskar belonged to us! When we questioned his actions, he stated that since there was no collar, he had the right to dispose of the cat. We celebrated a week later when he was fired for shooting someone's pair of Irish setters.

We've never forgotten our Oskar from so long ago. I'm sure he contributed positively to my children's upbringing, if not their sense of good humor!

Marcia Letzring is a retired psychologist, teacher, and municipal judge. She currently lives in Mexia, Texas.

Berman — By Jennifer Berman

CAT SCHOOL FINAL EXAMS...

Your owner is reading the paper <u>and</u> has a full bladder.
What do you do?
A. Sit on the paper
B. Sit on owner's lap
C. Tip over coffee mug
D. Sit quietly on the floor

OK... I KNOW I CAN RULE OUT "D"...

Homer's Odyssey—Taking the Country Out of the Cat

Bill Ott

I always avoided naming my cats after literary characters—way too pretentious in my opinion. Animals with names like Ophelia might as well as be forced to walk around with a sign hanging from their necks saying, MY OWNER READS BOOKS. So why do I have a cat named Homer? My daughter did it. If Homer has a literary antecedent, it's not the Greek poet, it's Homer Price in the children's book.

As if to live down his literary name, Homer established himself early on as a first-rate hunter, not only claiming the usual mice and birds but occasionally going after bigger game, too. I'm not saying Homer was responsible for the sudden disappearance of a neighbor's pet chicken, but there were those chicken feathers in our yard the day after the hen vanished. It happened rarely, but once in a while Homer got the worst of a tussle. Take that encounter with an irritable possum who left the overmatched Homer with a substantial portion of his jaw disengaged. Emergency surgery was required to set him back on the trail of "big game."

I was concerned about Homer's peace of mind a few years ago when I left the suburbs and moved to a loft in Chicago. How would Homer Ott, Critter Fighter, adapt to urban living? Quite nicely, as it turned out. Perched on the windowsill of my fifteenth-floor apartment, Homer likes to gaze contentedly at Chicago's western vista, as if he were a land baron surveying his property.

There is, however, a downside to the urbanized Homer. With little to do other than survey his property, he tends to get bored easily, thus requiring my attention. This is fine when I am home, but I travel frequently. Homer does not believe in the idea of travel. He abhors the sight of suitcases, and when he spots even a small overnight bag emerging from the closet, he invariably lodges a formal protest by urinating in it. I was always a procrastinator when it came to packing, but necessity has required me to take the concept of "last minute" to an altogether new level.

Bill Ott is the editor and publisher of *Booklist* magazine, the review journal of the American Library Association, located in Chicago, Illinois. Bill and Homer live in the Chicago area.

*No tame animal has lost less of its native dignity
or maintained more of its ancient reserve.
The domestic cat might rebel tomorrow.*

—William Conway
Archbishop of Armagh

Halston Versus Ian

Keith Madeleine

The sun is shining. It's a beautiful, lazy Sunday and I'm enjoying the warm sunlight coming through this picture window. Lately, my favorite place is on the top of the back of this plush chair. It's just high enough to see out the window, and wide enough for my eighteen pounds of cat fat. I feel my eyelids getting heavy. My tail swings with a carefree mind of its own as I gaze and think those thoughts that cats spend hours musing over. Humans can never understand how we cats can spend so much time doing nothing. Poor humans, they don't have a clue.

I really must be relaxed. There's a robin on the eave right above my head, and I'm not even getting worked up. I can never seem to get past the ledge without knocking my head on, what's it called, a "window?" After a while, a cat learns his limits. Fine, the birds can have the trees, I've got the furniture. Maybe I'll nap.

Oh no, I can hear those footsteps plodding my way again. This baby boy . . . this thing they brought home and is now walking, sort of . . . he just loves to terrorize my feline friend, Jasmine, and me. She's learned how to hide from him, but that's not my style. This baby and I are going to come to terms on my terms!

I hear the dad from the kitchen, "Ian, don't you dare pull on Halston's tail!" Too late, the little imp has grabbed a handful. My patience fails; besides, this time it hurts! I jump down from the chair with no grace at all to delighted squeals and giggles from the baby. I have had it. I have been tolerant, patient, accepting, everything they wanted, but I am not putting up with this pulling thing anymore. It is time to settle this once and for all.

I scoot across the room, turn, sit, and wait. This is going to be good. I haven't just been sitting there thinking about nothing, you know. I have been planning my strategy, and it's time to implement plan one. The kid totters, turns, and makes his way to my side of the room. He's actually getting around pretty well for only having two feet on the ground and all. Sitting on my haunches, I'm just about the same height as this little guy.

I sit so pretty, with eyes big and shiny. He can't resist coming at me. Just as he leans into his off-balanced stance to grab at me again, I let loose with a right hook that any boxer would be proud of. The room reverberates with a loud *smack* from my good-size, declawed paw. A perfect connection. He plops down onto his diapered baby butt with a look of total shock! Beautiful! I turn, flip my tail, let out a cocky meow, and strut away. He's not crying, just dumbfounded. The dad's in the hallway laughing like crazy, and I get the feeling he's proud of me for standing up for myself.

Well, one for the cat! That was work—kind of made me hungry. Think I'll just have a bite to eat and glower in my victory. Hey, the sun is on the chair in the kitchen now. I don't think my adversary's going to be bothering me anymore. I'm feeling quite victorious.

What a great feeling, lying in the sun, warming my thick black fur. I'm starting to doze and think those kitty thoughts. My tail starts to slowly swing as I nuzzle into myself. Maybe I'll even purr a little. My ears suddenly perk up—what's that I hear? . . . "Ian, don't you dare pull on Halston's tail again, you're gonna get it, Ian. . . ."

Keith Madeleine owns a unisex hair salon and lives
in Macomb County, Michigan.

My Kitty, My Parrot

Sandy Burgess

Most people who own cats won't own a bird of any sort, and vice versa, for obvious reasons. I seem to have inherited one of each; in fact, they are one and the same. If you're wondering whether I've somehow genetically created a cat-and-bird hybrid, I guess I should explain further.

Like most cat owners, I endeavor to keep my cat off all tables and especially the kitchen counters. Fortunately, Flower, named after the skunk character in *Bambi,* hasn't quite gotten the knack of leaping from the floor to the countertop, which isn't to say she hasn't tried various ways to get there. Some of her ways have been more painful than others, for her and for us.

There are three basic methods Flower has attempted to use thus far. Her first method, and probably the simplest and most logical, is to climb onto the counter via any chair that is left close enough so that she can jump from one to the other. This has proved successful, but we've gotten smart and don't leave chairs anywhere near the counters anymore.

Her second method of getting to this perch, still somewhat logical yet not so simple, is to try to scale the lower kitchen cabinets. She digs her claws in, leaving various pockmarks and scratches, and climbs up to the top drawer, where she extends a paw over the top, searching for something—anything, another ledge perhaps—to grab on to in order to anchor her claws and pull herself up to the counter surface. She has yet to find the final stronghold, although she keeps trying.

Her third method is why I refer to her as my parrot. She hasn't done this to me in a while, but if I was standing at the counter, occupied with something, and she was hungry or just plain curious, she would back up, make a running start, hit my lower back, and then spring onto my shoulder to peer over like Bluebeard's parrot. I would patiently walk into the living room, with Flower still on my shoulder, and place her on the couch. Many times she would come running in again. She did this until the day I roughly deposited her in a kitchen chair and scolded her because this time her claws had dug a little too deeply.

Although she has decided to leave me alone, mostly, she has surprised my mother with this! It was my mother's turn to host a card game with three of her friends. As she was preparing a luncheon—at the counter—this daring young kitty decided that Mom might be a little more tolerant than I was. My sister, who was also among the group that day, saw Flower preparing her attack run. Before she could get a "cat-pounce" warning out of her mouth, Flower shot off, and before you know it was up on my mom's shoulder peering down at freshly prepared sandwiches. Needless to say, my mother was caught quite off guard and let out a yell that could have awakened the dead! Flower was quickly and sternly removed from her perch.

Having discovered her aerialist abilities, Flower pretty much gave up on methods one and two, temporarily, and apparently was not yet finished with method number three. I could hear her mind at work: "Okay, so it doesn't work on Mom or Grandma. I haven't tried Grandpa yet!" Within a few days came Grandpa's turn. However, Grandpa wasn't at the kitchen counter when kitty tried her "parrot" impersonation, he was in the bathroom shaving! Flower just wanted an unobstructed view from high atop the perch on his shoulder. A running start . . . a flying leap . . . a spring up . . . then quickly down. Someone pass the styptic pencil!

Sandy Burgess has an accounting degree and currently works as a
legal secretary in the Juvenile Division of the Oakland County
Prosecutor's Office. She and Flower live in Pontiac, Michigan.

Prissy Adopts a Duck (Based on a True Story)

Lori Crews

Prissy Sissy With the Sassy Tail," queen of the Known Worlds, had taken possession of the home I once, unknowingly, considered to be mine. Over the course of time she had scouted out the entire neighborhood (this was back in 1975, when we lived on a dead-end country road with no traffic, so she was allowed out whenever she so desired). All the dogs were properly cowed into subservience to Her Majesty, and all the other cats bowed and scraped when she deigned to visit their poor abodes, graciously sharing their food and toys.

Just behind her house was a stable that catered to racehorses from around the nation, brought here to compete at the racetrack in nearby New Orleans. On the stable grounds was a pond, which served the needs of the local fowl life. Prissy, being a fastidious feline, never stooped to such crass behavior as chasing or attacking these visitors. Instead, she would sit on the back fence and watch their antics with a superior cat smirk, laughing to herself when a clumsy bird made a crash landing into the water.

One day in the late 1970s she noticed a mother duck walking around with seven little ducklings following along behind. Now, Prissy had never seen a baby duck before and decided to get a second look. The foolish mother duck mistook Prissy's interest for the stalking of a hungry predator. She let out a horrible, discordant quacking noise, fluttered her wings in agitation, and chased her youngsters into the water. In her haste, however, the mother duck left one of her ducklings stranded on the shore between Prissy and the water. Prissy walked over to the tiny bird and sniffed a bit, to define and catalog the new scent. She gave the duckling a few licks about his head. His mother must be awfully neglectful to leave one of her younglings so smelly and ungroomed!

Having once had kittens of her own, who were now grown to fine specimens of cathood, Prissy was most disturbed by this obvious negligence. She decided that this little being needed a proper mother—her own superior self! And since she no longer had the ability to have kittens, she thought this little creature would be a fine substitute. Prissy gently lifted the young bird in her mouth and carried him back to her home. She brought the duckling over to her favorite napping nest, set him down, and gave him a proper grooming. She lay down next to her new foundling and waited for him to snuggle up to her for a nice nap. Imagine her surprise when the errant youngster waddled over to her water dish and climbed in!

Oh, this poor wretch was not only uncared-for and ungroomed, but also woefully lacking in proper catlike behavior. The idea of splashing around in one's water supply! Prissy got up and gently swatted the babe out of the bowl and back to her nest, where she had to groom him all over again. After a while Prissy began to feel a bit hungry and, being a conscientious mother cat, got up to go and find something to bring back to the nest for her new baby.

She told the youngster, in the firmest tones of voice, to stay right where he was until she got back with some lunch. However, when she started to walk away the young scamp got up and followed along behind her! She turned around and head-butted him back into the nest and started to walk away, but the stubborn little thing just got up and followed her again. Oh well, she'd deal with this misbehavior another time when she was not quite so hungry.

I heard a familiar tapping at the back door, put down the book I was reading, and went over to let Prissy in for lunch. I was quite amazed when I saw a tiny duckling trailing her into the kitchen and over to her food bowl. Prissy stopped at the bowl and patiently waited for her adopted son to take his fill before she herself ate. She seemed quite perplexed when her new babe did not even give a sniff at the food. Prissy had never had to cope with a kitten who wouldn't eat—all her kittens had been voracious eaters.

She walked over and swatted a morsel onto the floor in front of the duckling, thinking that he might be used to live food and would want it to be moving before he feasted upon it. When this didn't work she looked up to me for help. I grabbed some bread from the pantry, broke it into bits, and put some into Prissy's water bowl. Prissy gave out a disgruntled meow and looked at me as if I had lost what little sense I'd had, but was even more astounded when her new kit gobbled up the bread from the water. After watching him eat for a while, she gave a little cat shrug and ate her own lunch.

After they'd eaten I decided I'd better find the duckling's birth mother and return him. I picked up the little fellow and started out the back door, Prissy at my heels meowing furiously at me to put down her kitten so she could give him a good after-lunch wash. I proceeded to the pond and spotted the mother duck on the opposite shore with her six little ducklings.

After putting the little fellow down, I picked up Prissy (she was anxiously trying to reclaim her lost kit), backed off quite a bit, and waited to see if the mother duck would reclaim her lost son. Sadly, mommy duck was not too swift in the brains department and had forgotten all about her missing child—she would have nothing to do with the youngster even after more than an hour of waiting. I gave a sigh and returned home with Prissy in my arms, hoping that the little fowl would be reunited with his family after I was gone.

Prissy, however, was not that dismissive of the situation. As soon as I'd set her down, she'd started running back toward the pond. I chased her down and brought her inside, hoping she'd forget about the duckling (oh, how foolish I was!). After listening to two hours of pitiful mewling and howling, I picked Prissy up and headed for the pond to see if our little visitor had found his rightful family. No such luck—the tiny foundling was hunched down at the edge of the water all alone. Who was I to try to mess with fate?

As soon as I put Prissy down she made a beeline for her new baby, picked him up, and ran back home to her nest. I walked over and looked down at her as she groomed "Quackers." (Don't groan, my kids were only three and four at the time—they're now in their twenties and were not very inventive in the naming of pets; witness Tigger, Fluffy, and Muffin, Prissy's last litter.) Prissy looked up at me accusingly and gave a small huff. When I bent down to get a closer look at Quackers she put her paw over him protectively and made a little growl to warn me that I'd better not try to take away her new kit again.

Well, it seemed we had a new addition to our family—one with feathers. Prissy reared Quackers as carefully and lovingly as she had her own birth kittens, and he grew to be a fine, healthy duck. It was quite the talk of the neighborhood to see Prissy sashaying down the sidewalk with her new kit waddling along behind her everywhere she went. Tigger, Fluffy, and Muffin easily accepted their new brother and taught him how to tussle and run with them during playtime. They never could quite figure out why he wouldn't share in their feasts of field mice, but what the hey, different strokes for different folks! They loved him despite his weird ways and always included him in their grooming and cuddling fests. There were times when I could almost hear Quackers purr!

Lori Crews is an Internet services customer analyst, computer programmer, writer, and artist who lives with her family in Houston, Texas.

I have studied many philosophers and many cats.
The wisdom of cats is infinitely superior.

—Hippolyte Taine

Cross-Country, Truck-Driving, On-the-Road Kitties

Belinda Sauro

L ife was pretty normal for me in 1988. I lived in Washington State with my four kitties, had a job, and met Mike, my future husband, at his parent's dry-cleaning business where he worked. In 1995, he decided to leave the dry-cleaning business to find something that paid more money. We learned of an opportunity for Mike to go to truck-driving school in Missouri. It sounded like a fun adventure and both of us were ready for a change, so we packed up our belongings and our four kitties, and headed south. Little did I realize the journey that lay ahead of us.

Once we were established and Mike was in school, I decided to get a full-time job as a greeter at the local Wal-Mart store. There were two entrances to this particular Wal-Mart. I worked one end and a friend of mine worked the other. On one particular evening, I had to escort a customer to the service desk, which was located at the other end of the store. As soon as I walked down to that end, a cat walked in. My friend said, "Oh, you like cats. Why don't you take him home with you?" Already having four cats, I didn't dare bring another one home.

I picked him up and took him deep into a wooded area behind the building to let him go. Of course, that allowed me just enough time to fall in love with him. He was one of those cats who just melted in your arms when you picked him up. I put him down and he followed me about halfway back, then he headed for the tire center, which I found out later is where he had been staying for about two weeks. Within ten minutes, though, the kitty walked back into the store and a cashier brought him to me. My boss, a kindly soul, let me take my break early so I could take him home. I kept him in the bedroom in case he was sick. Mike was on the road and wouldn't find out about our new family member for a few days—just enough time to have the kitty checked out and possibly find a good home for him.

When Mike got home, he was pretty understanding about the new kitty and let him stay, provided that it wasn't a permanent situation. He wouldn't have anything to do with the kitty because he didn't want to get too attached if we weren't going to keep him. It quickly became obvious to both of us that this kitty wasn't going anywhere, though, and eventually Mike grew to love him as I did. We named him Bailey. When Mike was away, the kitties and I would keep each other company. The weather in Missouri can get rough, and on stormy nights we would all curl up on the living room floor, cat carriers nearby, in case an emergency exit was needed.

Bailey the cat on the road again

After about eighteen months of life in Missouri, I told Mike I was homesick and bored and didn't want to live there anymore. We decided to move our now seven-member family back to Washington. The question was, How were we going to get the kitties there? We weren't going to fly them or put them in cargo, so the only option was to bring them with us and our belongings in the extended-cab part of Mike's truck. We decided to make an adventure out of it by taking time to haul cargo to various places, while wending our way back.

We spent three fun-filled

months together on the road with our kitties. First, we had to rig a curtain separating the cab of the truck from the sleeper area so that we could put the kitties back there when we had to get out. I did this by putting a bar at the bottom of the curtain, poking holes all along the edge, and putting shower curtain rings in it to connect it to the bar. This allowed us to pull the curtain shut (it Velcroed down the front) so we could leave the truck to eat, shower, do laundry, and not worry about the kitties escaping. We had air conditioning, heat, and lights, so the kitties were very comfortable.

This worked for a while, until two of our kitties figured out that if they pushed hard enough they could squeeze under the bar. Imagine our surprise one day when we came back to the truck and found two little kitties sitting on Mike's seat waiting for us. Well, Mike got on the passenger side of the truck and distracted them, while I opened the driver's side door (with my eyes on them the whole time) and jumped in. It was scary because I was always afraid one of them would dash out. Thankfully, this never happened. Eventually all the cats got into the act and I'm convinced they delighted in seeing how rattled we were when they were sitting there waiting for us.

The kitties pretty much had free run of the cab while we were driving. Two of them liked to lie on the dash and tell Mike how to drive, while another claimed the top bunk for hers and sat in front of the TV when we watched before going to bed. (We had a satellite dish on the truck and could watch anything we wanted.) Another kitty liked to lie across Mike's shoulders and watch the scenery go by. You can only imagine some of the looks we got from other drivers on the road! The kitties seemed to enjoy the adventure, and why not—they were showered with attention for three months.

Life finally returned to normal after we moved into our apartment. The cats mostly play happily together, Mike only drives locally so he's home more, and I am in school to become a travel agent.

Belinda Sauro lives with her husband, Mike, and five kitties
in Tacoma, Washington.

Emergency Vets to the Rescue

Robert Taylor, D.V.M.

In my twenty-eight-plus years in practice as a veterinarian I have seen some pretty amazing rescues of all sorts of animals—some made it, some didn't. Most are brought to our emergency vet hospital in pretty bad shape. The little victories gained from saving an animal's life definitely give us motivation to continue our work. Certainly, all of them have touched our hearts. Two recent successful cat stories truly define why we do this type of work.

The first happened recently. A good Samaritan came upon a little gray kitty crawling along the curb on a busy street. He was literally pulling itself along with his front legs while dragging his hind legs. Upon closer examination, it was clear that both of the cat's femurs were fractured, and the bones had been driven through his skin. The bones were badly contaminated with dirt, mud, hair, fecal material, and a variety of other things. The kitty had been like that for probably several days, judging from how devitalized the tissue and the bone appeared.

The woman who brought the kitty to us, as it turns out, has a son who is mentally challenged. The child, just in the short time that it took to bring the kitty over, was intrigued and developed an immediate bond with the kitty. When we went in to examine the kitty, it was just an amazing thing to watch him trying to purr on the examination table despite the injuries that he had. This was obviously a wonderful kitty.

We felt that this poor kitty had been through such a traumatic ordeal that he deserved another chance, and he had already used up one of his lives. So we undertook the process of repairing the fractures and rehabilitating the kitty. It took several operations and extended aftercare to put him back together correctly. Of course, the little boy and his family visited the hospital regularly to check on the kitty. Once he was healed enough to be handled, we were able to give the kitty to the family. The little boy was thrilled. Now, years later, the family still has the cat. We have a special fund here at the hospital to which the staff and clients donate; it paid for the entire treatment.

The other story that comes to mind is of a cat who was burned quite badly. Unfortunately, cats sometimes fall prey to children or mean-spirited individuals who will cause them harm. Some years ago a group of children were catching cats and literally torturing them. The cat who was brought in had been burned when gasoline was poured over her back and ignited. The cat was black and white and had little white tips on her ears, and the ears were burned right down to where they were only about a half an inch high. There was also a large burned area that extended from between her ears back to the end of her tail.

We were able to rehabilitate the cat through some operations. But the thing that struck me most was this cat's personality. From the very beginning she seemed to understand that we wanted to help her.

Due to the circumstances of the cat's injuries and subsequent recovery, there was quite a bit of local media coverage. Of course, this brought a flood of people who wanted to adopt the cat. In fact, we had over one hundred names of people who wanted to take the cat, including several of our own technicians. We finally decided that the only fair way to place the cat was with a lottery. One of the women who worked in our laboratory was chosen from all the names.

The cat is doing very well. Her burns all healed and all of her hair grew back, and other than the short ears, you would never know she had been injured. It's a happy ending for a cat who had had such a tough beginning.

There are a hundred other stories just like this one. I guess the thing that's remarkable about cats is that they seem to know how to take of themselves. We see many who are seriously ill or severely anemic—instead of 50 percent of their cells being red blood cells, they come in with maybe 8 percent. Many animals, especially dogs, couldn't survive being this anemic. Cats, on the other hand, seem to intuitively know that they need to be very quiet—very still—and almost go into a vegetative state. They are truly amazing animals, for many reasons.

Robert Taylor is a D.V.M. practicing at Alameda East Veterinary Hospital in Denver, Colorado, diplomat of the American College of Veterinary Surgeons, and the author of three animal books. The hospital, established in 1973, is the home of *Emergency Vets,* the highest-rated TV show on the Animal Planet channel, a division of the Discovery Channel.

How you behave towards cats here below determines your status in Heaven.

—Robert Heinlein

Ten for the Price of One

Gordie and Colleen Howe

Our cat story dates back to the mid-1960s. At the time, Gordie was playing for the Detroit Red Wings and our kids were young. Like their dad, they had a keen interest in hockey. One hot summer day I decided to take the kids and some of their friends out for ice cream. We were deciding what to buy when one of the kids noticed a cat walking in the middle of the road. They screamed for me to rescue the cat before she got hit by a car, so I ran out and retrieved her.

Gordie and Colleen Howe

She was a beautiful Siamese and seemed to be okay. She had no collar. We soon realized that she was very pregnant, as evidenced by the large bulge in her stomach area. The kids fell in love with her and pleaded with me to take her home. Somewhat reluctantly, I agreed. We named her Ming-Toy. She appeared to be quite healthy and took to the kids right away. (Obviously she had been around kids before.) She was a kind cat and always there at the door to greet us when we came home. To be fair to the previous owner, we put up signs and passed out flyers. No one claimed her and, much to the kids' delight, we decided to keep her.

Well, one night, not too long after that, we had to go out. When we returned home and she didn't greet us at the door, we knew something was up. We fanned out to look for her, but she was nowhere to be found. Finally, we spotted her behind the big couch in the living room, with nine newborn kittens, the same number Gordie wore on his jersey! Oddly enough, not one of them was Siamese! At that point I had no idea what we were going to do with them. We certainly wouldn't turn them out, and it would be a while before we could give them away.

Finally, the day came to find new homes for all of them. We came up with a cute plan to give each one away that would make it hard for anyone to resist. We found nine hat-size boxes and poked holes in each.

Next, we wrote notes that were supposed to look like the cats had written them, inked up one little paw on each cat, and pressed the paw print onto the notes. We put one cat and one note in each box and took them to various homes in the neighborhood. We set one box on each porch, rang the doorbell, then hid behind a bush or something to wait for the results. We were careful to choose homes where kids lived.

At each home the result was the same. The kids would take one look at the kitten and ask their parents if they could keep it. Surprisingly enough, not one was turned down. For the longest time the neighbors never knew we were the ones who had done it.

Gordie Howe is considered hockey's greatest all-around player of all time. His career spanned six decades and his level of playing is unprecedented in all sports. Colleen Howe is president of Power Play Publications and Power Play International, Inc.

A Grizzly Feline Friendship

Dave Siddon

My father always seemed to have a knack with animals, especially wildlife. He was a hulking 6'4" and 240 pounds, and I suppose the animals respected that. As far back as I can remember, he would take in stray injured animals and treat their wounds so they could return to the wild one day. It wasn't unusual to see him working with red-tailed hawks, Kodiak bears, mountain cats, hummingbirds—all sorts of North American wildlife. He would get calls from all over the Pacific Northwest about injured animals. He never said no and never charged a dime. In a year he treated as many as twenty-five hundred injured animals.

In 1981, he officially started Wildlife Images, a nonprofit animal rehabilitation center. Some years later the center started an "Animals to School" program to teach kids about caring for and preserving our nation's wildlife. I worked for a zoo some distance away and would come home on the weekends to help out.

In 1995, we were caring for a grizzly bear who had been struck by a train as a cub five years before. Griz, as we named him, is probably the gentlest, sweetest bear you ever saw, and totally unfit to be returned to the wild. The bear enclosures we installed for him are very secure for human safety, but cats and other small animals have easy access. Although bears generally eat nuts and berries, they will eat meat as well, so we watch the cages closely.

Someone had abandoned four kittens at the center, three of whom we caught and gave to good homes. The fourth kitten, simply called Cat, seemed to escape us at every turn. One day, while we were feeding the animals, the six-week-old kitten appeared in Griz's pen and boldly approached his food. There was nothing we could do but watch. We thought for sure that Griz, well over 650 pounds, would swat the kitten, and probably try to eat him. But as Griz sat there with his five-gallon pail of mixed fruits, vegetables, and meats, something remarkable happened.

He picked out a piece of chicken, stripped the meat from the bone, and presented the meat to the kitten. We were shocked! Later that day we saw the two of them cuddled up together sleeping, Cat safely tucked underneath Griz's front leg.

The two have become best buddies. Cat will ambush Griz and Griz will give Cat rides on his back. The pair have actually been good for the center—donations and attendance have both risen dramatically since word of their unlikely friendship has spread. Griz and Cat still enjoy each other's company and have now been joined by another stray cat.

Dave Siddon is director of Wildlife Images Rehabilitation and Education Center in Grants Pass, Oregon. Dave took over at the request of his father, who died of cancer in 1996.

Animals are such agreeable friends—they ask no questions, they pass no criticisms.

—George Eliot

A Cat Dynasty Reincarnated

Eve Hannigan

It's my belief that cats reincarnate, and, if they develop strong and mutual love relationships with their humans, will come back again and again to the same person or family. There has been too much evidence in my life to believe otherwise. It started when I was a small child and continued well into adulthood.

I remember waking up in the early brilliant April sunlight to joy and contentment when I was two and a half years old. My adored big sister was right across the room in the big bed, and through the slightly open sliding door between our bedrooms I could hear my parents breathing as they slept. All was right in my world. By that time, there had already been a cat in my life for four months. And I have no doubt whatsoever that Purry's presence amplified my contentment to the level where that morning became a permanent part of my memory.

My father had always had dogs, and my mother had never had pets, so having a cat was new to both of them. I think it was frustrating to Mother because she didn't like messy pets. When we moved into our house in Oceanport, Mother often swept the kitchen floor. To judge by Purry's occasional reaction, she'd clearly been hit with a broom to chase her out of the house.

Nonetheless, Purry endeavored to win Mother over. Our instant love of the cat, I'm sure, had something to do with Mother's turnabout. Also, the cat purred a lot; at five and a half, my sister named her "Purry." Thus began a thirty-year cat dynasty, one of three in my life.

In the early days, my sister and I weren't very good at telling boys from girls, so when Purry had Farmer Gray, we gave the kitten a boy name. And by the time Farmer Gray became obviously pregnant, the name was too well entrenched for us to change it.

Farmer Gray produced dozens of kittens over the next eight or nine years. She was a very relaxed cat who always had her kittens in a partially closed cardboard box under the old high chair in the kitchen, usually while we were attending. She notified us each time that births were imminent by pacing from one end of the piano keys to the other, turning around at each end on the little flat square of wood. She never did this at any other time, and she always did it just before retreating to the box for the start of each birth. The sight of her turning with her huge belly on that itsy-bitsy little square of wood at the end of the piano will stay with me forever!

Among Farmer Gray's progeny were Big Jon and Sparky, Solid Rock and Frail Flower, and Blackitty and Grackitty. Big Jon allowed us to hold him and splint a broken hind leg to a piece of plywood we'd cut and carved to the right shape and size. He never bit or scratched us even once during the process, though I know we must have hurt him, and he thanked us by recovering full use of his leg.

Solid Rock was a huge relaxed male with a great sense of humor and fun. His sister, tiny, delicate Frail Flower, had one tiny kitten—in Mother's lingerie drawer! We always figured she was a true southern belle and just too refined for cardboard boxes. By the time Farmer Gray had Blackitty and Grackitty, we'd run out of people to give our kittens to and names for the ones we kept. We called them "Black Kitty" and "Gray Kitty" until the amalgamated versions began to roll off our lips.

Blackitty (solid black) had a love affair with Goldie (marmalade orange) from three houses down. They were constantly together, usually at his house, but sometimes at ours. And unlike every other mama cat we had, when Blackitty had her kittens, it was in Goldie's garage. Goldie guarded Blackitty while their kittens were tiny, and they continued to be inseparable.

Blackitty was hit by a car and killed one night about a year later. Her all-black body was almost invisible against the blacktop surface of the street. But Goldie sat in the middle of the street beside her while cars whizzed by on either side, watching over her until we discovered what had happened and carried her body home.

Grackitty was lean and sharp and smart—and loved canned asparagus! We put our cats outside at night and didn't keep a litter box in the house, so when she needed to go, she'd ask to be let out. If we didn't respond immediately, she'd stand up on her hind legs and rattle the knob on the back door. And if we *still* didn't respond, she'd just slip into the little toilet room beside the back door, squat on the seat, and urinate in the toilet!

When I left my parents' home, I lived at college and in several places where I couldn't have cats. But as soon as I moved into a place where I could have pets, I got a kitten. Then I went back for her sister. Then I took in a beautiful, charming, pampered, purebred Siamese mama and a mere domestic shorthaired papa who'd managed to invade her citadel at just the right moment.

I have a special place in my heart for certain male cats, of whom Big Jon was the first, Rock Solid the second, and Golden Boy the third. Golden Boy taught me that combining a Siamese with an alley cat produced smart, funny, calm, and beautiful cats. He was all black, with absolutely gorgeous golden eyes, hence his name. But he eventually became known as Lumpy because, after performing a ritual greeting, he would ecstatically slide off my lap like a lump of lead. He didn't seem to care what body part hit the floor first, or how hard—if he'd been on my lap getting loved, relaxation was all!

One of Lumpy's offspring, Copy Cat, was a carbon copy of Lumpy, but in gray. We lived on a twenty-three-acre farm for a while. Every morning, Copy Cat would ask to be let out. Fifteen minutes later, she'd ask to be let in and would proudly sit at my feet with a field mouse in her mouth. She'd wait for compliments, then eat the mouse and ask to be let out again. She'd do this three times in a row. I guess three field mice make a great meal.

We had lots of room on the farm and consequently lots of cats. We were trying to give some away, having exceeded even our capacity for cats, when it looked like all *four* females were going into heat. We decided to keep them inside, but one of our males, Alex, who was less than six months old, managed to impregnate all of them!

I am convinced that Lumpy was Big Jon come back to me five or six years after Big Jon was hit by a car. About seven years after Lumpy disappeared, he came back to me in the form of a cat we named Java. He was also black and had that sweet, smart, funny nature common to the other two. He was full grown when he came to us, and the best-mannered cat I've ever known. He never begged or clawed or meowed for handouts—just sat composedly at our feet, politely, not even *looking* eager, and gently took any table offerings we held out.

At that time, we lived in a house that had a large louvered window over the stove and counter beside it. In nice weather, we'd take out the bottom two panes so Java could go in and out that way. Our wall oven was beside the window, and when we baked chicken, we never had to time it. Java would show up and stick his head in through the window *exactly* one hour and fifteen minutes after we put the chicken in. It was invariable.

Earlier, we'd lived in a flat in San Francisco. One nice Sunday, we were going down our front steps, and four or five of our neighbors were coming out of their houses, too. We saw Java up the street, and called to him. Heads turned everywhere, and one by one our neighbors said, "Oh, that's *your* cat? He's nice. He comes in and eats butter off my counter." "He does that in your house?" offered another. "He does that in mine, too." And so on. In our house, he never got up on the table while we were there, but if we left the butter out and uncovered, he'd have eaten it by the next time we looked!

Java was an amazing cat. He was utterly unafraid of dogs. There were German shepherds up the street from us who would sometimes venture down our driveway. Java would arch his back and make his fur stand on end, then make a stiff-legged sideways stalk up the driveway toward the dog. If the dog stood his ground, he got his nose bloodied! I once watched a small dog spot Java on the front fence beginning to rise in defense of his yard. The dog stopped, cocked his head, and carefully crossed the street. Obviously, he'd experienced Java before.

Java was quite physically attuned. Sometimes I'd begin to worry about him because I hadn't seen him in a number of hours. This would start as a vague, nagging little worry, and gradually progress to a more conscious one. A number of times this happened when I was out back in the garden. When the worry had gotten to a conscious level, I'd look up, thinking I'd seen him, but he wouldn't actually be there. Five minutes later, he'd appear exactly where I'd imagined him. It's like he was sending me messages saying he was okay.

Java was hit by a car and killed some time later. That night I dreamed over and over of seeing Java hit, and of finding Java after he'd been hit. I must have had twenty dreams about his death that night. I believe Java was reincarnated into Norman Schwarzenegger, this time in only about three years. Normie was huge, even as a kitten. He was part Siamese, black and white, beautiful, and had more soul in his eyes than any average gathering of angels.

Once when I was away, my husband was lying on the bed with Normie on his chest, talking with me on the phone. We joked around about Normie. Finally, I said, "Oh, just put him on the phone so I can say hello." So Steve held the phone to Normie's ear, and I began to talk to him the way I did when I was home. And damned if he didn't meow his special "I love you" meow and begin to purr loudly!

Normie caused us to coin the term *voice petting* because we could make him purr from three thousand miles away just by talking to him over the phone.

Normie left us a couple of years ago, disappearing just as Lumpy did. I miss him still—often quite acutely—and am waiting impatiently for him to be reincarnated into my life.

———————

Eve Hannigan is a writer as well as the publisher and editor of *Test Engineering and Management* magazine. She lives with her family in Oakland, California.

The Tale of Felis

William Schwedler

I am Felis, or cat to you. Yes, I will condescend to allow you to call me cat, which, of course, is not my true name. The *Homo sapiens* you know as T. S. Eliot knew of the fact that our true nature is the genus *Felis.* He was aware that our true name is known only to us. Yes, cat will serve well enough.

Before I can begin my story, I must debunk some long-standing myths. It has been rumored throughout the ages that we have nine lives in *each* incarnation, but having used that ninth life, we are, in fact, reborn. In truth, there is but one life in each incarnation. The total number of cats is finite. We have always been and always will be. Another popular myth states that when we fall we always land on our feet. If that was totally true, some of us would have very short legs. No, we have the ability, through our superior intelligence, to know when to land on our feet, when to land and roll, and when it is time to move to our next incarnation.

Oh yes, our intelligence is superior beyond question. Name another species, I challenge you, who can communicate all wants and needs with a single word: "Meow!" What expression, force, and nuance we can put into that single word! Those of you *Homo sapiens* with whom we have deigned to reside can educate the others—those we have found unqualified to be our servants and companions. Know this: The relationship between cat and all other species must be clearly understood. We are here to rule, you to serve. Do it well and faithfully and you will prosper. Mistreat or ill use us at your own peril!

As stated earlier, we have always been. *Homo sapiens* anthropologists have written that genus *Canis* was the first domesticated animal. Of course this is true, since canines need humans to survive. We felines, on the other hand, have never been and never will be domesticated. We merely choose to behave in whatever manner suits our purpose. We will lie on your lap and allow you to caress us and tell us how wonderful we are.

Certainly; why not? We also honor our faithful servants by bringing them gifts of mice, birds, rabbits, and whatever comes to tooth and claw. It must be human feelings of unworthiness that so often bring about such negative responses to our gifts.

There is no doubt in my superior mind that we are the least understood of God's creatures. Of course, some of your human predecessors recognized us as the godlike creatures we are.

Around 2600 B.C.E. is the time you humans reckon we first began to live among you. Is it a coincidence that this was at the beginning of what you call civilization? Not really. We could see that Egyptians needed help uniting the upper and lower kingdoms and administering a growing empire. We chose to pass along some ideas to the pharaohs, and in return they gave us the proper respect, even mummifying our castoff bodies after we passed to our next incarnation. We aided in Egyptian prosperity by drastically reducing the populations of rats and snakes plaguing the Nile Valley. Other nearby peoples such as the Assyrians and Hebrews actually ignored or viciously attacked us, no doubt out of jealousy for what we had accomplished in Egypt. Moses was upset when Pharaoh said, "You and your people may leave Egypt, but you may take no cats with you." Poor Hebrews!

Ancient Greeks wanted to import some of us from Egypt, but when the Egyptians refused, the Greeks stole some kittens. Our arrival in Greece brought peace and culture; not only did we subdue the rat population, but we inspired Socrates, Plato, Aristotle, and others as well. What is known as Greek philosophy is really cat philosophy. The Greeks were good listeners.

Human anthropologists and archaeologists have long pondered why no bones of cats were found when Pompeii and Herculaneum were unearthed. The answer is simple: We were smart enough not to reside on the slopes of an active volcano!

Another of your human sayings is that "curiosity killed the cat." Please, give us credit where it is due. Were it not for feline curiosity, Europe would not have been civilized, nor later America. The commanders of Roman legions were led north, east, south, and west by their cats, who wanted to see what was beyond that river, over that mountain, behind that tree! The legions followed the cats and conquered. An interesting side-bar to this is that none of the conquered peoples had been treating cats properly. I warned what would become of ill use or mistreatment. Yes, our curiosity helped conquer and civilize the world.

Columbus, Cabot, Drake, Verrazano, Hudson, and all the others knew better than to sail out to sea without a cat. We were their inspiration. When you've been at sea for weeks with nary a tree on which to sharpen your claws, or a bird or squirrel to stalk, you will use all your skills to help find land. We cats can always sense where the nearest land lies, and by running to the part of the ship closest to land, we signaled the captains to follow our wise and timely counsel and change course.

Yes, I am Felis, or cat to you. All that I have related to you is true. Cats do not lie, except to lie in wait. (A cat joke. I don't expect you to understand.) But what I ask of you is unqualified respect for our species. The next time I lie in your lap, listen to me! Is that a contented purr or an important message?

William Schwedler taught at Mumford High School in Detroit, Michigan, for thirty-two years. He now writes, acts, and directs with local theaters.

If man could be crossed with the cat, it would improve man but deteriorate the cat.

—Mark Twain

Flying Feline

Patty Johnson Cormaney

If there's anything the cat hates, it's a honking house. To put this a little more clearly, Samovar the cat goes off like a Roman candle when the smoke alarm does. My husband, Elmer, installed the smoke alarm in our trailer as a special precaution after we'd read about several RVs that had burned to a cinder. We've had a fire extinguisher for years but we decided it was time to add a smoke alarm as well.

The trouble is that in a travel trailer, space is worth its weight in platinum, so Elmer put the smoke alarm on the hall ceiling. It seemed like a fine idea at the time, but apparently the smoke alarm felt neglected all alone there in the dark hall. So every time I opened the oven door when I was baking, the smoke alarm let out a blast that not only could wake the dead, but did arouse the occupants of neighboring trailers to the point of madness.

This is nothing compared to what it did to the cat, who was able to hear mice a mile away, and therefore had ears as finely tuned as Jack Benny's violin. Every time the smoke alarm pierced the silence, the cat grew forty feet of fur in all directions, leaped into the air, and headed for the bedroom. After I turned on the air conditioner to clear the air and my eardrums, I would look for Sam.

He was always in the bedroom, of course, because that was "about as fur as he kin go." But by that time, he would be huddled up in a corner so small you could scarcely see him with the naked eye. It took about thirty minutes to cool down the kitchen and calm down the cat. The last time all this happened, Elmer lay back on the couch and laughed so hard I thought he'd start the smoke alarm up himself!

"You should have seen this one," he said. "When the alarm went off, you were just about to take the roaster out of the oven. You were so scared, you raised one leg, made a slow half turn, threw the oven mitt on the floor, and said a four-letter word."

"Oh, I couldn't have!" I cried. "I'm a lady. I don't swear." Elmer swore I did, though. He laughed a long time about that one.

The one who was most annoyed, though, was the cat. The night the smoke alarm went off three times before I could get a meal on the table, he was flailing his way through the trailer faster than a speeding bullet. And every time I went to the bedroom to console him, he told me what he thought in growls and hisses. I understood him perfectly. Sam was no lady.

That seems like such a long time ago now. Sam passed away some years ago at age nineteen, which is surprising since the smoke alarm probably took nine lives and more. We always had Persians and other elegant cats. Currently, though, a large, stray calico named Kate keeps me company. I got her from the Humane Society. I named her Kate after one of my favorite actresses, Katharine Hepburn.

Our relationship didn't start out very well. We had always owned male cats. Kate was also the only one we didn't get as a kitten. The vet at the Humane Society estimated that she was about five when we rescued her. It took six weeks for us to form a bond, which was actually more like a truce. We've finally come to an understanding, though. Over the three years since she came to live here we've grown quite attached to each other. Kate had a rough early life, having been sideswiped by a car and then abandoned. But now she seems to be enjoying life, and enjoying being the queen of the household.

Patty Johnson Cormaney is a retired writer who wrote for several publications and had a regular column in *Trailer Life* magazine. She currently resides in Cedar Falls, Iowa.

Tiger: Once a Predator . . .

Michael Bouchard

Our family moved from Michigan to Texas when I was very young because my father was transferred there as part of his employment with Chevrolet. While there, we got a gray-and-black-striped cat we named Tiger. He was as normal as any other cat, except he ran sideways. Anywhere, everywhere, and at any speed, he would run sideways. We always wondered if his back end would beat his front to where he was going.

After a couple of years we moved back to Michigan, and eventually Tiger passed on. We got another cat similar to Tiger in color, whom we named Tiger II. (Some in the family preferred Tiger Too, but he was my cat and I said his official name was Tiger II.)

Tiger II grew up to be a good-size cat and loved to have fun. We fed him regular cat food, but his favorite food was chicken and chicken scraps. My parents didn't approve of handing down food from the table, so we had to give him the scraps in his bowl. He always knew when chicken was being prepared. He would stand by the stove, sit under the table, rub up against someone's leg, and occasionally meow.

As it happened, my brother, Jeff, was also a fan of chicken. Well, one night my mother prepared chicken for dinner. Jeff took the biggest piece, a breast, and put it on his plate. He must have spent well over ten minutes trimming away the fat and skin, and removing the bones, until all that remained was a big, beautiful, perfectly trimmed piece of chicken.

He paused for a moment and glanced up at us with a gloating look on his face, obviously proud of his perfect piece of chicken. Big mistake! Just as he was about to enjoy his prize, Tiger II stood on his hind legs, jumped up on Jeff's lap, and grabbed the chicken breast. Before Jeff could react Tiger II ran upstairs. Jeff raced after him like he'd been shot out of a cannon, all the while yelling at the cat to return his chicken, but it was too late.

Tiger II dashed under the bed out of reach and ate the whole piece of chicken before Jeff could stop him. Jeff was steamed, while the rest of us laughed until we had tears in our eyes. After that, Jeff was very careful about how he ate his meals, especially chicken. For a long time, whenever Tiger II was anywhere near the table, Jeff's posture was that of a boy guarding his food from a predator. Hey, once a predator, always. . . .

Michael Bouchard is a Republican state senator in Michigan,
representing much of southern Oakland County. A former police
officer, he was first elected in 1991.

Are cats lazy? Well, more power to them if they are. Which one of us has not entertained the dream of doing just as he likes, when and how he likes, and as much as he likes?

—Fernand Mery

Cat Fact Quiz 5

Hodgepodge

TRUE OR FALSE
1. Cats live longer indoors than out.
2. Cats have an excellent sense of direction.
3. Cats damage their feet each time they jump from place to place.
4. Cats age more in their first year of life than in any other.
5. Some cats have six toes on one or both feet.

ANSWERS
1. *True.* The average life span of an indoor cat is approximately four-teen to sixteen years, and only three to four years for an outdoor cat.
2. *True.* Cats have a homing ability that uses the earth's magnetic field, the sun's angle, and their own biological clocks, all of which give them excellent direction.
3. *False.* Cats have specially designed foot pads that absorb the shock of landing.
4. *True.* A one-year-old cat is similar in age to an eighteen-year-old human.
5. *True.* Some cats are born with extra toes. This is called polydactyly.

See if you can guess who these celebrity cats might belong to.

1.

2.

These drawings were done by artist John Harrow.

3.

4.

5.

Give up?

1. *Clint Eastwood*
2. *Pamela Anderson*
3. *Michael Jackson*
4. *Madonna*
5. *Sylvester Stallone*

Her Highness, Marble, and Curious George

Karen Benton

I grew up around all sorts of animals. Our house had the usual assortment of cats and dogs, plus one parakeet who made the fatal mistake of thinking he could land on dishwater suds. Also, my grandparents had a farm and apple orchard, so there were all sorts of barnyard animals to play with. Currently, we have two cats and a dog. In some people's estimation this makes me a cat person, simply due to majority rule. In my estimation, however, I am just a soft touch, whose house would be overrun by any cat, kitten, dog, or puppy who needed shelter. My loving husband is understanding about my love of animals but has informed me of the certain disintegration of our happy home if I do take in every stray that finds its way to our door, so I am content with the animals we have.

As with most owners of animals, I have many tales of joy as well as pain from my years of companionship. My two favorites are about the acquisitions of my cats. The first to join us was Marble. Now eighteen, she's a gracious old lady who holds court when she wants. My eldest daughter, Ariel, also eighteen, was nine months old and crawling when the sitter's cat had kittens: two longhairs and two shorthairs. I valiantly resisted my sitter's pleas for a worthy home for one of them, but the day I picked up my daughter and saw her pulling a six-week-old fur ball backward—and the kitten *not* clawing at the chubby little baby hand firmly fastened to her tail—was the day I changed my mind. The kitten was resisting by digging her claws into the carpeting but kept losing ground until she hit the linoleum, at which point she was ignominiously pulled into my daughter's lap and remained there quietly.

I was impressed by the kitten's fortitude, but when she started to purr, my first thought was that this cat must like pain! She disproved that thought within three days of joining our family when she demonstrated the course that her discipline of a too-rough baby would take. If leaving the area didn't work, my daughter received a kitten slap on the side of the head! This method worked great for the cat until my daughter was two. By that time, the force of the slap had grown to involuntary claw extension on impact, and Marble one day actually left a scratch. I made a conscious decision to never let Marble out, except on a leash, so I had her declawed in the front. Marble continued to administer a well-deserved slap now and then, which taught my daughter to be somewhat gentler.

While Marble has since discovered that discretion is the better part of valor and only sometimes deigns to honor us with her presence, Curious George is another story. George is a twelve-year-old orange shorthair who literally clawed his way to the top—of my shoulder, that is! For a time, I worked out of my mom's home office. Her cat had kittens and they, of course, had the run of the house. I quickly learned to always watch my feet when I came in the door for fear of stepping on one or being attacked. One of the orange twins was noticeable in his attachment to me; no matter where I was in the house, he was at my feet.

Pretty soon, he was standing up on my legs for pets and scratching, and it didn't take long for him to climb my jeans to my waist. When the time came for adoption, I didn't hesitate. Any cat who shows such marked partiality for someone shouldn't be parted from that person. While at my mother's house, George was true to his name, since he was the first kitten to go under and behind the stove, refrigerator, desk, sofa, and other hard-to-reach places. I was not surprised, therefore, when he got himself trapped behind the wall in the under-stair closet within the first fifteen minutes of arriving at my house. We ended up knocking a hole in the wall for him to get out. Hence the name Curious George!

Marble, then six, and a lifelong only cat, did not appreciate this obnoxious kitten. She proceeded to give George lessons on proper behavior with the appropriate smacks, but gave it up when I bought a collie pup named Jack. Marble had a protector in Jack, because the dog seemed to stop George from bothering her. This is how Marble learned to accept both new babies' rowdy, rough-and-tumble plays for attention. I would separate them from Marble only when her slaps to Jack's head were of sufficient force to echo down his nose.

George didn't seem to mind much that Jack was a dog. Maybe he just didn't realize there was a difference, since they grew up together. They were best friends, while Marble seemed to watch them from the shadows. If Jack wasn't carrying George around by the head, George was leaping on Jack from above. They turned the whole house into a play area and race-track. In July 1997, though, the years caught up with Jack and he had to be put down. We buried him under a favorite tree in the backyard. George sensed everything, and was given the opportunity to touch noses one last time and say farewell, which he did. It took us all a few weeks to adjust, with Marble showing greater progress than the rest of us.

Karen Benton is a 911 police dispatcher and lives with her family
and pets in Oakland County, Michigan.

Confront a child, a puppy, and a kitten with sudden danger;
the child will turn instinctively for assistance,
the puppy will grovel in abject submission,
the kitten will brace its tiny body
for a frantic resistance.

—Saki

Muffin's Man

Liz Mulligan

Capricia told Muffin everything. She talked to her as though Muffin could understand. Many times Muffin reacted as though she did, in fact, understand, like a silent therapist helping Capricia arrive at conclusions to problems in her everyday life.

Though silent (as many therapists are), Muffin was peculiar in ways that would have perplexed even Freud. She ran all around the apartment, stalking Capricia and attacking her feet. Few human counselors resort to such playful tactics, but these idiosyncrasies brought Capricia much pleasure. She delighted in her cat's feisty energy and sense of surprise.

Capricia made efforts to get out and be social, but her involvement always seemed short term. Muffin made sure of that. Capricia joined a bowling league and met a young man there. She invited him over to play cards. Muffin entered the room and sniffed his feet. She then ran away, arching her back and hissing. The young man followed the cat and attempted to pick her up. Muffin let out a howl and darted from his arms.

The rest of the evening the visitor was on red alert, while Capricia looked upset. He said, "Nice cat," but kept his distance. Capricia's fate seemed to be that of an isolated woman whose youth was slipping away all too quickly. When the young man left, Muffin pranced around as though she had achieved a victory. Muffin was territorial. She had claimed Capricia as her own, and no one was going to interfere with her turf.

"What am I going to do with Muffin?" Capricia moaned. This

episode was repeated again and again. Capricia invited a man over to play cards, and Muffin did her territorial dance. The man got nervous and Capricia never heard from him again. As much as she loved Muffin, Capricia needed contact with other humans. She didn't want to choose between her cat and a date; she wanted both.

One night after bowling, Capricia met a nice-looking, polite, and rather shy man at the snack bar. They chatted a little bit, awkwardly at first, and eventually warmed up to each other. Capricia invited him over the following evening. "Okay," said the young man, "but I'll warn you, I'm allergic to cats." Capricia's heart sank. She felt her entire social life was doomed because of the cat she loved so much. "I could put Muffin in the other room," Capricia offered timidly.

"Well, I guess it would be all right. I'll see you tomorrow."

Capricia kept Muffin in the bedroom while the young man was there. She wondered why she hadn't tried this approach earlier. It solved a lot of problems.

The couple were playing cribbage when they heard pawing at the bedroom door. The noise grew louder and was soon accompanied by rumbling. Somehow, Muffin managed to get the bedroom door open. Capricia put her hands to her face as she watched the scene develop.

The young man tried to fend off the cat, but Muffin, sensing his disinterest, landed on his lap and stayed there the whole night. Capricia was worried her friend might have a severe allergic reaction, but he seemed to be doing fine.

Muffin purred on his lap as though the two of them were the best of friends. He slowly reached to pet her, and she responded with an outstretched chin and closed eyes. He pulled a treat out of his pocket for the content feline and gently set her down.

He admitted that he'd seen Capricia at the bowling alley and asked about her. He found out she had a jealous cat who served as her confidante and thought if he told Capricia he was allergic to cats, Muffin would warm up to him. The reverse psychology worked. Capricia and her clever friend were soon inseparable.

Liz Mulligan is a writer whose story of Muffin first appeared in *Cats* magazine in December 1997.

Crazy for Kitties!

Kathy Lawryk

I was in the U.S. Navy during my second tour of duty in Hawaii when I met Mouser, my Hawaiian cat. She was a tiny, tiny kitten who wandered into my roommate Pat's workplace. I believe it was in January 1979 when Pat came home from work and told us about a little kitten that he had been keeping at work. He told us it was going to get chilly that night (remember, we're in Hawaii now) and he didn't want the kitten to get cold and maybe become sick. So he asked if he could bring her home. He added that even as tiny as she was, she was really good at catching mice. Well, Chris (my other roommate) and I each had one or more cats, so we said yes. I suggested the name Mouser, since she was such a good one.

Chris and her cats eventually moved out. Soon Pat also moved out, but he didn't take Mouser with him. I adopted Mouser, and along with my other two cats, Smokey and Bandit, we became a family of four. Several years later, Smokey developed a brain tumor and had to be put down. Then Bandit got sick and had to be put down as well. That left only Mouser to keep me company.

I eventually got married to a wonderful man named Mike. We were stationed at Keflavík, Iceland, as our last duty station before I retired from the navy. While we were in Iceland, Mouser stayed home in Alabama with my brother.

Mike worked for a security company and one of his (terrible) jobs was to pick up stray cats and dogs. If nobody claimed the animals within twenty-four hours, they were taken to the local vet and destroyed. Well, one day a stray cat call came in and my husband was sent to investigate. When he got to the little kitty, she latched right on to him. He called me later that day and told me what was going to happen to the little kitty. I really didn't want another cat because I had Mouser waiting back home in Alabama.

Much to my surprise, Mike brought the cat home with him that night, and, being the softie that I am, I fell for her almost immediately. When she let out that first squeaky sound, I was hooked and we named her Squeekey. We got her in September 1992, and she's been with us ever since. She adapted quickly to life in Alabama when we returned home.

In the first week of July 1997, our vet told us that Mouser was getting on in years and wasn't going to be around much longer. The thought of not having her around, sitting in my lap, was just too much to bear. Not that any kitty could ever replace Mouser, but still, I wanted to find a new kitty to hug and have sit on my lap like Mouser. I called our city animal shelter and the lady there said they had just gotten a very loving, affectionate kitten; I should come take a look at him. She said that someone had stopped by the side of the road, opened the car door, and just put this little kitty out.

We went to the shelter right away. The lady there (her name was Donna) took us into the back, where the cages were. She opened the cage, took out a little silver-and-gray-striped kitten, and handed him to me. It was love at first sight! He was the cutest, talking-est kitty I had ever seen! He had the loudest purr I had ever heard, too. We filled out the paperwork and took this little "motorboat" to our vet to be checked out before taking him home.

We kept him in a separate room the first couple of nights, since I didn't know how Squeekey and Mouser would react to him. Mike slept with him in the guest bedroom the first night and then I slept with him the second. We made sure all the kitties would be okay together before I let him have free run of the house.

We kept trying to come up with a name for him but nothing really seemed to fit. It took us two weeks to finally settle on one. He was into everything—doing all kinds of crazy somersaults—a real "little rascal." So that's what we named him. And, believe me, the name suits him to a tee.

A short time later, we called our city's shelter again to see if any more kitties were available. Donna told us she had gotten two kittens in the night before. They weren't kin but had been strays at the same house and had been brought in together. She said one of them had the strangest markings she had ever seen. "She looks just like a little ragamuffin," Donna said.

We went to the shelter that afternoon. Donna took out the little calico kitten and handed her to me. She was so tiny, and most of the fur was gone around her head and neck. Donna said it was probably due to scratching fleas. The other kitty in the cage looked *exactly* like Squeekey, except he had more coloration on his face. I picked him up and held him. He looked just like a fox in the face, the way his coloring was. He was very loving, too. But we were only going to take one.

Donna had us sign the paperwork but didn't charge us the normal $5 adoption fee because she was happy that this little orangish ragamuffin kitty was going to a good and loving home. We decided to name her Muffin.

When we left, I felt bad about not taking the other kitty, especially because he had been with Muffin for so long. And the thought of him being destroyed the next day made me feel even worse. As we drove off from the shelter, I told my husband how I felt about taking Muffin away from her friend. I also said it was really sad that he was going to be put down the next morning.

My husband, being the wonderful man that he is, said we could get the other kitty if I wanted to. I called the shelter from the car phone and we went back to get the other kitty. I decided that since he looked so much like a fox, we would call him Fox. Donna was happy because now she wouldn't have to put down any kitties that week.

We went home and introduced Fox and Muffin to Rascal, Squeekey, and Mouser. At first the cats didn't want to have anything to do with the new kitties—but that didn't last long. Fox and Muffin have been good playmates for Rascal and Squeaky. Sadly, Mouser didn't get to know her new pals for very long. She suffered from bad arthritis and kidney problems. In September 1997, after eighteen years of friendship, she was put to sleep. Except for losing Mouser, we are all just one, big, happy family.

Kathy Lawryk retired from the navy and is now a Web page creator and graphic designer. She lives with her husband, Mike, and a houseful of cats in Eufaula, Alabama.

No matter how much cats fight,
there always seems to be plenty of kittens.

—Abraham Lincoln

Cat Proverbs

Happy is the home with at least one cat.
—Italian proverb

Beware of people who dislike cats.
—Irish proverb

A cat is a lion in a jungle of small bushes.
—Indian proverb

Those that dislike cats will be carried to the cemetery in the rain.
—Dutch proverb

Give Me Your Tired, Your Sick, Your Homeless . . .

Luanne Cooper

There are cat people, and there are *cat people.* I am of the latter persuasion, the kind who can't say no to a kitten or cat in need. I grew up around cats and that love has certainly carried through to adulthood. Ironically, my mom now lives with me and my bevy of feline friends.

The first cat my husband and I got was Mickey. She was a lovable cat and looked just like one my mother had when I was younger. At the time we lived in an apartment that didn't allow pets. We hid Mickey pretty well, covering her cage with a tablecloth when anyone came over. No one ever suspected. We would take her to my mother's house during the day, transporting her in a shopping bag so as not to look conspicuous. I'm sure the neighbors wondered why we did so much shopping and what on earth we could be buying so much of. Eventually, though, Mickey was discovered by someone in the apartment building, so off she went to live with my mother. She was used to being with her during the day anyway so it was an easy transition. Mickey lived to be twenty-one.

Our cat collection began to grow when we moved out of the apartment and into our own home. We were bicycling through the new neighborhood when we found a tiny kitten walking by the side of the road. We carried her home in the basket that was attached to my bicycle. The next one came when we were visiting a friend's horse farm. A kitten was running around behind the horse on the horse track, which is dangerous for more than one reason! She was extremely friendly and jumped up on my shoulder when I bent down to pet her. We decided it would be better and safer for the cat if we took her home.

We found more as the years went by—mostly kittens who were hungry, lost, or injured. Our home seemed to be a magnet for cats in need, sort of a feline halfway house. One male we got came from a garden center. The center's own cat had a litter of kittens, who were all given away except for our male, because he had a huge hernia. We took him and paid for the surgery as well. The garden center owner wanted us to take the mama cat also, and we agreed. We had to wait to pick her up, though, until the male kitten recovered from surgery. It was a happy reunion for both.

Some years ago we moved to Wisconsin for a while, cats included. We lived near some docks and railroad tracks. One day when we were exploring we found a very tiny kitten who was covered with tar and obviously quite undernourished. No one we talked to thought she would live; nonetheless, we took a chance on her, slowly nursing her back to health, and she lived to be nearly twenty-two years old. I've always believed that cats have a strong will to survive, and this cat was a perfect example. We used traditional as well as some homeopathic methods to treat her. Many vets won't use or recommend homeopathic treatments, but I know they work.

Having owned as many as fifteen cats at one time, all strays, I've seen my share of hilarious and touching incidents, as well as had several triumphs. Billy is one triumph I'll never forget. We had moved back to Michigan by this time, buying a house that sits on a little over an acre of land. Billy, as we named him, wandered near our house and just seemed to stay there. I began feeding him, and for a year he lived outside our house, appearing every day for a meal. He wasn't the type of cat who wanted contact of any sort with me or probably anybody else. He learned quickly, however, that before he got his meal, I was to be allowed to pet him and scratch his head. The minute he finished his meal, he wouldn't let me near him. Smart cat!

One day Billy came home with a very badly infected foot, no doubt the result of a fight with another animal. As usual, he wouldn't let us come near him, so we had to trap him to get him to the vet's office. He

Sheeba eating her twenty-first-birthday doughnut

ended up having the toes amputated on the injured paw. The vet said that if any more time had passed he may have lost a leg, or worse. Ever since then he's been one of the nicest cats we've owned. He stays indoors now and follows me around wherever I go. We had to trap another cat, Tommy, when he came home with two legs injured on the same side. Because of the way the bones were damaged, the vet said he had obviously had a run-in with a bigger animal. Despite the vet's concerns that Tommy might lose both legs, he healed nicely and is still with us.

One of the funniest moments I had with my cats is when I held a birthday party for them. There were only three with us at the time. My husband and I loaded the cats in the car and drove to the local five-and-dime to buy party hats and other things. I asked the woman at the counter if the store had any small party hats. She remarked, "Oh, someone's having a birthday. How nice." I said they were for my cat. She just sort of stared at me in disbelief. I said I was serious and pointed to my husband in the car with the cats hopping about with bows around their necks. She looked at me and said, "Why do I get all the cuckoos at my register?" We put the hats on the cats and fed them catnip cupcakes.

I'll never forget the time an insurance salesman came to our home to try to sell us some insurance. We put all the cats in one room and shut the bifold doors. As we sat at the kitchen table talking, the cats started to get rather rambunctious in the next room. They were bouncing around, banging on the doors, sticking their paws underneath, jiggling the door handles, and generally making noise that sounded like horses galloping far away. We sat there the whole time trying not to laugh out loud. Certainly the insurance man could hear the noise and could see the amused looks on our faces; nonetheless he sat there, expressionless, diligently going through his routine. He never called or returned after that. Hmmm. I may be on to something here!

Once one of our neighbors watched our cats while we were on vacation. When she came in to check on them and feed them one night, she noticed that all the cupboard doors were open, and one was even off its hinges. She was scared that our house had been broken into, so she called a neighbor to help her search it. They looked high and low, but couldn't find anyone or anything missing. The cats had simply found a way to open the cupboards to do a little investigation.

I can't explain why I take in so many stray and injured cats, other than to say that I simply love them. My husband, Ken, has been very patient and understanding with me. He is very fond of them, too. My mom, who lives downstairs, also has a cat. Many times when one or two of our cats tire of playing with the others upstairs, they'll travel downstairs for some solitude. It's kind of like a kitty day care. And just like parents who can tell their kids from a hundred others in a noisy room, I can identify my cats by their meows. Perhaps I was put here to be a friendly haven for cats in need.

Luanne Cooper lives with her husband, Ken, and an
ever-growing family of felines.

How Jordan Got Cats

Jordan Orzoff

I've always considered myself a cat hater. No cat in particular, just in general. Sneaky clawed little bastards, y'never know when one is going to shred your skin or something. And they don't *sit* and *come* and *roll over* like dogs.

But I digress. . . . Where was I? Ah yes, a few days after Christmas 1993, I had just returned to Minneapolis from Chicago. I was taking care of business, doing laundry and such. As I made the trek from my apartment to the laundry room, I noticed a large white-and-gray cat parked against the utility room door—just lolling there—not doing much of anything. Since I lived off an indoor hall, this was odd, but I ignored the cat. (I had years of practice!)

I made trek after trek, bringing the whites, bringing the darks, bringing more quarters, bringing some of that static cling stuff. With each trip I made, the cat had edged a little closer to my apartment door. Well, I wasn't a doctoral student for nothing—I could see the writing on the wall. On my last trip, I made a dive to close the door—*whoosh!* The cat was inside.

I opened the door. "Cat, get out!" I yelled. He didn't respond to my voice commands, or the open door. I might as well have been a piece of early Cubist art for all the interest the cat had. He proceeded to make himself thoroughly at home, exploring every nook and cranny of the apartment. (For the record, it had three nooks and a cranny and a half, plus a walk-in closet.) My long-squelched sense of generosity came into play, and I figured that this was a stray cat and I might as well take care of him until his owner claimed him. Now, I was vaguely aware that cats eat from little cans that cause them to sing "meow" along with a bouncing ball and that they do something gross in a litter box, but that was about it. However, like most people on the planet, I have at least five hundred close personal friends who are cat owners. I called one.

Amused by my panic ("It's in the bathtub! What do I do now? It's rubbing its head against my leg! Help!"), she instructed me in the Care and Feeding of Unwanted Cats. I proceeded to make an 11 P.M. trip to the grocery store for cans of cat food (leaving me in the bizarre position of standing in the aisle debating the merits of fisherman's stew versus liver nuggets), a plastic pan, and Scoop Away Clumping Cat Litter (which I bought because it comes in a milk gallon container and is thus comfortingly familiar, even though I won't drink it).

I returned, warily, to the apartment. The cat was still there. I placed the pan on the floor, poured litter into it, and stepped back. The cat approached the pan, scratched at the litter, but walked away. I opened a can of cat food, wrinkled my nose in revulsion, and set it down. The cat set upon it like he'd never eaten before. Instant bonding.

I placed an ad with the local Humane Society (very nice people, by the way), posted signs on all the entrances to the building, and waited. The cat grew increasingly attached to me and even ripped up the carpet next to the door anytime I dared lock him out of the bedroom or bathroom. My damage deposit began to shrink. I decided the cat needed a name, so I called him Pirate because of the large gray patch over one eye. Little did I know I had identified his personality.

Over the next few weeks, Pirate became increasingly territorial. Friends came over and tried to coo over the cat, but left my apartment in fear because he hissed and clawed at anyone who came in—except for me. Me, he wanted to sleep with. (It reminded me of some relationships I've been in.)

A month passed. Nobody claimed him. Pirate accompanied me to the vet to get shots. The vet thought Pirate was adorable, but it still took three people to hold him down for the injection. In my first attempt to mellow Pirate's personality, I got him neutered. (This taught *him* to come wandering into my apartment uninvited, and should give any of *you* pause before you drop by my place—heh heh heh!) No such luck, however. Pirate continued to worship me and attack guests. After three months, as a sign of my continuing mental deterioration, I went to the Humane Society to get a friend for Pirate.

Josie is a tiny black-and-white "tuxedo and mittens" female who absolutely adores every single person she has ever met or ever will meet. She and Pirate get along pretty well, but Pirate is still mean to people.

Four months after Pirate moved in, his owner showed up. He lived next door to me. He kicked the cat out of his apartment ("for some air") and was glad when he didn't have to let him back in. Tales of Pirate's kittenhood made me suspect the prior owner was a cat abuser. It's every psychologist's dream—past trauma revealed as indicator of present countersocial behaviors!

Advance another four months. A friend's cat had kittens. I was resolute in not taking one until I actually saw them. Lucky, a gray-and-white tabby, joined our household. Despite being roughly one-sixteenth Pirate's size, Lucky proceeded to stake his dominance no more than two days after arriving. Pirate and Josie have great fun with Lucky. Lucky keeps the other cats away from the pounce treats. Pirate celebrates by taking a flying, hissing, clawing leap at my next guest. Life goes on. . . .

Jordan Orzoff, Ph.D., is an industrial and organizational psychologist who works in training evaluation for Motorola. He and his three cats live in Palatine, Illinois.

I love cats because I enjoy my home; and little by little, they become visible soul.

—Jean Cocteau
French poet and filmmaker

Cathyrose Celebrates Christmas

Mary Witkowski

Cathyrose lives in a house that is warm and cozy. She is a playful cat and is Pamela's favorite pet. "She's my best friend," says twelve-year-old Pamela. It is nearing Christmastime, a merry and joyous time of the year. All day long, Cathyrose watches as Pamela bakes some cookies. Finally, the last batch of cookies is cooling. Until now, Cathyrose has been able to suppress her temptation. But the sweet smell of cookies filling the air is becoming too enticing for Cathyrose and she's beginning to lick her lips. Just one cookie, she thinks, just one little, broken cookie. Who would want a broken cookie? Me! I do!

The telephone rings. Pamela has to leave the kitchen to answer it. Ah, here's my chance, thinks a quick-minded Cathyrose. With one nimble reach, she paws a broken cookie. Mmm, how good it tastes! I'll dip my paw in this glass of water to wash it down. Pamela will never miss one broken cookie.

When Pamela returns to the kitchen, she immediately notices a cookie is missing. "Cathyrose!" Cathyrose knows she has been caught. Pamela admonishes, "Cathyrose, what makes you think you can get by stealing a cookie?" But Cathyrose just licks her lips and blinks her eyes and purrs. Pamela smiles . . . she just loves Cathyrose.

Cathyrose is very playful. Pamela and she play hide and seek and peek-a-boo. Pamela hides behind a door and soon she'll see the tip of Cathyrose's ear, then the side of her forehead comes into view, and last of all an eye will appear as Cathyrose sneaks to stalk her prey. Out leaps Pamela shouting, "Peek-a-boo," and Cathyrose's eyes pop out like a balloon.

Pamela talks to Cathyrose. (She says Cathyrose understands everything she says.) She asks, "Do you want to talk? No?" Then Pamela will say, "There's a new kitty cat next door." Now Cathyrose perks up, for she doesn't understand, and she doesn't want to share Pamela's love with that neighbor cat. "Let's watch television," says Pamela. "It's time for the animal and bird show you like." When the birds go "tweet-tweet" or "chirp-chirp," Cathyrose leaps to the television screen. Then she turns and looks at Pamela, for the birds have disappeared. Where'd they go? she seems to ask. When the commercials come on, Cathyrose turns around and softly curls up on the couch.

After playtime and television time, Cathyrose will want to go to sleep. It's don't-bother-me time. Pamela sits on the sofa, and suddenly, up leaps Cathyrose to burrow and snuggle beside her. After a brief spell, Cathyrose springs off the sofa and climbs up onto a chair, rests her head on her paw, lets her hind legs drape limply off the seat edge, and purrs herself to sleep.

Now it's time to clear the table and put those cooled-off cookies in Christmas boxes and have some dinner. When Pamela places the teacup on the table, up vaults Cathyrose onto the chair. She sits upright and places one paw daintily on the table; the other front paw rests on top of her first one. She is ready to be served her cat chow. To tease Cathyrose, Pamela will drop a newspaper on the table in front of her and say, "Read the local news to me while I cook dinner."

After dinner Pamela shows Cathyrose the Gingerbread House. Last year there was a "mouse cookie" inside. Cathyrose remembers this and wonders if this year she will find another mouse cookie. She's wise and patient and cunning and knows everything will happen on Christmas Day. "It's time to hang your stocking," says Pamela. "I'll take your picture." Pamela is always taking pictures. When Cathyrose sees the camera, she thinks, oh no, not again!

It has been a busy day. Pamela and Cathyrose are tired. It is time for a good night's sleep. "Ho-hum, I'm sleepy," says Pamela. She climbs up into her soft and comfortable bed. Cathyrose looks up and Pamela pats her on the head. "I remember the Christmas when I found a little kitten in a red wicker basket purring for attention. What a merry Christmas! That was you, Cathyrose." Now Cathyrose climbs on the bed and cozies up near Pamela. Soon they will be in dreamland.

The following morning they awake before daybreak, just like all the children do on Christmas Day. "Meow, meow," says Cathyrose. "Look what Santa Claus left for me! Just what I asked for. Look at all those trolls!" She sniffs the trolls one by one, and when she purrs, Pamela knows Cathyrose is enjoying a merry Christmas. (There is a mouse cookie in the Gingerbread House, which will be a surprise for Cathyrose later on.)

Opening packages soon becomes monotonous to Cathyrose, especially after she's opened all of hers. She scampers off to a solitary retreat where she can nestle up comfortably. Maybe she wants to give Pamela a chance to open her presents. (Cathyrose gave Pamela a cat book titled *Tricks Cats Play on People.*)

Cathyrose is about to retire when she sees a new ball of green yarn. Hmmm, that ball is about to be unraveled. "Prrrr, Prrrr! Christmas is such fun!"

Mary Witkowski is a writer of children's stories who lives in Moorestown, New Jersey. This true story first appeared in *Hopscotch for Girls* magazine. Mary is a former designer of Caribbean clothing.

Purring is an automatic safety valve device for dealing with happiness overflow.

—Anonymous

The Grapes of Cats?

Sally Keys

Anyone who owns cats knows that the cats run the household. What I haven't figured out, though, is how the cats determine their division of labor regarding daily chores. I have been puzzling over this recently regarding my own two felines, whose direction I have been under for the past six years.

I had been catless for a long time, and then came Winston. He is a beautiful black-and-white "tuxedo" cat who was named after Winston Churchill due to the following shared characteristics: He is small, stubborn, likes high places, does not like to be ignored, and has a *big* vocabulary. I did not know that I would be away as much as it turned out I was, so I decided Winston needed an associate. That's where Punk came in. He is an all-black darling with captivating green eyes who earned his name by standing up to Winston when he first arrived. He is a cat with attitude. But the name *punk* really does fit him, because he is sort of a coward who protects Winston as the smaller of the two. Both of them seem to have developed an effective job division strategy.

For example, it's Winston's job to open closet doors, while Punk handles the bathroom doors. Of course, they open doors only when the space is occupied; if unoccupied, then they shut the doors with themselves inside—with predictable results. This keeps the household running in the way they deem most fit.

It's also Winston's job to make Sally wake-up calls, while Punk is in charge of solo aria performances. Winston has another allotted task, which escapes my memory for the moment, but it balances Punk's compunction to keep all inhabitants of the household clean—including me!

I still haven't figured out, however, who has the assigned duty of removing the hanging bottom bauble from my metallic grape-leaf chandelier. When I moved into my home, I thought the light fixture was ghastly—metal leaves intertwined with glass balls (or other beadlike dangles) for grapes—but upgrading that particular interior decoration was not on my immediate list of things to do.

The cats, however, had other ideas. One day I came home to find the bottom round bauble off the chandelier and resting on the glass table, which was at least four feet below it. My first questions was, How? My next question was, Who? And my third question was, Why didn't the table break? I was puzzled for a while but then resolved to leave the conundrum to minds more agile than mine. I figured it wouldn't happen again, so why worry?

Then I came home another day—only to discover the bottom round bauble off the chandelier and resting on the glass table again. The other baubles hung in their designated places, but the bottom one had apparently been as carefully removed as the first time, and the table was no worse for wear.

I have had suggestions from friends to set up a cat burglar camcorder cassette to capture the guilty party in action, but I prefer to think of this as simply one more division of labor in a household affectionately ruled by my four-footed friends, Winston the Vociferous and Punk the Irresistible.

Sally Keys is a children's protective services worker.

Of all God's creatures there is only one that cannot be made the slave of the lash. That one is the cat.

—Mark Twain

Kevin Debastos

Brittany Lain

Desiree Tucker

Brandon Kay

Marianne Price

Selected cat drawings from Ms. Seller's fifth-grade class at Our Shepherd Lutheran School in Birmingham, Michigan

Eric Endlich

Alex French

Fiona

Max the Cat. Drawing by Fiona Dohanyos, age 9

The Cat and the Fox

From Aesop's Fables

Once upon a time, a cat and a fox were talking politics together in the middle of the forest. The fox said, "Let things turn out as badly as they will. I do not care, for I have a thousand tricks for the enemy before they can hurt me. But pray, Mrs. Puss, suppose there should be an invasion, what course will you take?"

"Nay," said the cat, "I have but one course to take, and if that won't do then I am certainly done for."

"I am sorry for you," replied the fox, "with all my heart, and would gladly furnish you with one of mine; but as times go, it is not good to trust. We must be everyone for himself, as the saying is, and so your humble servant."

These words were barely out of his mouth when they were alarmed by a pack of hounds that came upon them. The cat quickly ran up a tree and sat securely among the top branches from whence she beheld the fox, who, overtaken with his thousand tricks, was not able to get away and was torn in as many pieces by the dogs who had surrounded him.

Moral: A man who boasts of having more cunning than his
neighbors is generally a silly fellow at heart.

The Cat and the Mice

From Aesop's Fables

A certain house was infested with mice, until one day a cunning cat came to live there. The cat caught and ate some of the mice each day. The mice, finding their numbers growing thin, consulted among themselves as to what to do about the preservation of micekind and the jaws of the devouring cat. They resolved that no mouse should go down below the upper shelf.

The cat, observing that the mice no longer came down as usual, became hungry and disappointed. She thought to herself how she might entice them within reach of her paws. Thinking that she could pass herself off for a bag or for a dead cat, she suspended herself by the hind legs from a peg, in hope that the mice would no longer be afraid to come near her.

An old mouse, who was wise enough to keep his distance, cautiously peeped over the edge of the shelf and said, "Many a bag have I seen in my day but never one with a cat's head. Hang there, good madam, as long as you please, but I would not trust myself within reach of you even if you were stuffed with straw."

Moral: Prudent folk never trust him a second time,
who has deceived them once.

Rainbow Bridge

Anonymous

Just this side of heaven is a place called Rainbow Bridge. When an animal dies who has been especially close to someone here, that pet goes to Rainbow Bridge. There are meadows and hills for all our special friends so they can run and play together. There is plenty of food, water, and sunshine and our friends are warm and comfortable.

All the animals who have been ill and old are restored to health and vigor; those who were hurt or maimed are made whole and strong again, just as we remember them in our dreams of days and times gone by. The animals are happy and content, except for one small thing; they each miss someone very special to them, who had to be left behind. They all run and play together, but the day comes when one suddenly stops and looks into the distance. His bright eyes are intent; his eager body begins to quiver.

Suddenly, he begins to run from the group, flying over the green grass, his legs carrying him faster and faster. You have been spotted, and when you and your special friend finally meet, you cling together in joyous reunion, never to be parted again. The happy kisses rain upon your face; your hands again caress the beloved head, and you look once more into the trusting eyes of your pet, so long gone from your life but never absent from your heart. Then you cross Rainbow Bridge together. . . .

Final Thoughts

Franklin Dohanyos

In listening to many cat owners while writing and editing this delightful, eclectic collection of feline stories, I've learned that cats are, without a doubt, the most "humanlike" animals on earth when it comes to personality and demeanor. That fact alone probably explains why most people equate having cats to having kids. I've witnessed firsthand people talking to their cats as if they were two-year-old toddlers, cooing and gurgling with them as if the cats actually cared. It's obvious that people draw a sense of purpose from owning a cat, and also a well-known fact that people who have cats often live a longer, more peaceful life than those who don't.

One thing I've observed is that people love to talk about their cats, every story being funnier than the last. And just when you think you've heard the very last story, there's always the statement, "Oh yes, I forgot to tell you about . . . ," or "Oh, I just remembered the time that. . . ." It's not so much that every cat owner is long winded, it's just that cats do so many quirky, hilarious, and heartwarming things that there's always something to talk about.

Overall, I think the best thing about cats, and all animals in general, is that they're nonconfrontational. They don't belong to any political parties, have no religious affiliations, don't follow sports, don't drive, and don't start wars over a piece of land. That's not to say that *people* don't argue or fight about whose cat, or which cat, is the best of the breed. But the cats themselves don't really care. Of course, cats may argue with other cats, but that's an entirely different story. After all, one cat must respect another's space.

Franklin Dohanyos

Franklin Dohanyos owns an active publicity and writing services firm in Oakland County, Michigan. He previously coauthored the widely popular book *Zuzu Bailey's "It's a Wonderful Life Cookbook,"* filled with over two hundred mouthwatering recipes, plus trivia, photos, and stories from the movie *It's a Wonderful Life.*

Franklin lives with his wife, two children, and cockerpoo dog in Oakland County. He enjoys hockey, writing and playing music, and Renaissance art and music. Although the Dohanyos home is "catless" at this time, Franklin's favorite breeds are the Scottish Fold and the Maine Coon.